Octave Feuillet

The diary of a woman

Octave Feuillet

The diary of a woman

ISBN/EAN: 9783337202002

Printed in Europe, USA, Canada, Australia, Japan

Cover: Foto ©Raphael Reischuk / pixelio.de

More available books at **www.hansebooks.com**

THE
DIARY OF A WOMAN

FROM THE FRENCH OF

OCTAVE FEUILLET
AUTHOR OF "THE ROMANCE OF A POOR YOUNG MAN," ETC.

NEW YORK
D. APPLETON AND COMPANY
549 AND 551 BROADWAY
1879

HE who signs these pages is, properly speaking, only the editor of them. How they came to be intrusted to him, how he was authorized to publish them, what modifications of detail were imposed upon him, are questions for which the reader will care little if this autobiography interests him, and still less if it does not.

O. F.

THE DIARY OF A WOMAN.

PART FIRST.

May, 1872.

WHEN I was at the convent, my quarterly re-
ports almost invariably ended with this definition
of my moral person : " Happy character, judicious
mind, gravity beyond her years, well-balanced nature. Conscience, however, a little uneasy."

" Conscience a little uneasy "—I do not deny it;
but as to the rest, asking pardon of these ladies, I
must be allowed to assert the direct opposite. As
my beloved instructresses were mistaken, it is not
astonishing that the world should be deceived also.
I fancy that the cause of these false judgments is
my external appearance. I am a dark brunette and
pale; my expression, of a tiresome unchangeability,
is as severe as that of a young girl can be. Some-

what pronounced near-sightedness lends a look of
sleepy indifference to my black eyes (whose brilliancy
would without this troublesome circumstance certainly be too striking). Besides, I have naturally a
calm manner of speaking, walking, sitting, and of
moving noiselessly, which gives an observer an illu-
sory impression of tranquil serenity. I have neither
the desire nor the means of correcting the opinion of
the public in this respect; and, until there is a new
order of things, my locked diary alone will know
that this grave, wise, and well-balanced Charlotte is
at heart an excessively romantic and impulsive young
person.

And this is precisely why I am so late in beginning this magnificent locked diary, which was bought
with enthusiasm three days after I left the convent,
and has waited three years for my first confidences.
Twenty times have I seated myself before its white
pages, burning—like King Midas's barber—to intrust my secrets to them; twenty times my "uneasy
conscience" has made me throw aside my pen. This
conscience said to me that I was about to undertake
an imprudent and foolish thing; that the habit of
recording my impressions, of analyzing my emotions,

of nursing my dreams and giving a body to them, would have one inevitable consequence — that of bringing to the surface those romantic and passionate depths which are dangerous to a woman, which might prove fatal to the repose and dignity of my life, and which I ought rather to force myself unceasingly to suppress and extinguish.

Something my grandmother said this evening has, thank Heaven! removed these scruples. We had had some people to dinner. Afterward we played the game of " secretary," which consists of writing questions on slips of paper, folding them, and shaking them together in a basket; each player draws a question by chance, and replies to it as best he may. But one of our guests, a young deputy who prides himself on his profundity, always managed in some way to keep his own question in order to reply to it the more brilliantly. On one occasion he asked himself, " What kind of a woman best performs her duty? " I was charged with the collection of the little slips, and I read his question and at the same time his reply, which was worded thus: " The woman who best performs her duty is one who does not seek romance in life, for no real good comes of it; who does not seek poetry in it, for duty is not poetic; who does not seek in it passion, for passion is only a polite name for vice."

A concert of flattering murmurs, in which I had the cowardice to join, greeted this elegant maxim, during which the author betrayed his *incognito* by a modest smile. He was disconcerted, however, by an exclamation from my grandmother, who had abruptly suspended her netting. "Oh! oh! pardon me!" cried she, "but I cannot let such heresies pass before these young women. Under pretext of making dutiful women, would you make fools, young puritan? In the first place, I do not understand this mania for always opposing passion to duty —passion on this side, duty on that—as if one were necessarily the opposite of the other. But we can put passion into duty, and we not only can, but ought; and I would even say, my dear sir, that this is the secret of the lives of virtuous women, for duty all by itself is very dry, I assure you. You say that it is not poetic. That is certainly my opinion, but it must become so before any one can take pleasure in it; and it is precisely in rendering vulgar duty poetic that these romantic dispositions, against which you hurl your anathemas, serve us. If you ever marry, choose a woman who is not romantic, and see what will come of it."

"What will come of it?" said the young deputy.

"Well, it will turn out that everything in her life will seem flat and insipid—her husband first, if you will excuse me; then her fireside, her children, even her religion. Ah! surely it is not against romantic ideas that the present generation has need of guarding itself, my dear sir, I assure you; the danger for the moment is not there; we do not perish from enthusiasm, we perish from platitude. But to return to our humble sex, which is alone in question: Look at the women whom they talk about in Paris —I mean those whom they talk about too much; is it their poetic imagination that blinds them? Is it the search for the ideal that misleads them? Ah, great Heaven, three-fourths of them have the emptiest brains and the barrenest imaginations in creation! Ladies, and especially you young ladies," added my grandmother, " believe me, do not fetter yourselves. Be enthusiastic, be as romantic as you choose. Try to have a grain of poetry in your heads; you will be the more easily virtuous and the more sin-

cerely happy. Poetic sentiment at the fireside of a
woman is like the music and incense of a church;
it is the charm of right living!"

So spoke my dear grandmother, God bless her!
and that is why I have opened my precious locked
diary at midnight, and why, in peace with my conscience, I dare say to myself, "Good-night, romantic
and impulsive Charlotte!"

May 20*th.*

Yesterday I was in my boudoir, torturing my
piano and perfecting myself in my vocal exercises,
when Cécile de Stèle, my friend from childhood and
my dearest companion at the convent, rushed in like
a whirlwind as usual, seized my hands, turned her
two rosy cheeks to me, and said, in her vehement
and affectionate way, "Charlotte, are you always
and ever my dear sister, my guide, my support, my
little spiritual mother, my golden heart, and my ivory
tower?"

"Why this litany, dear?"

"Because you can do me an immense service.
Fancy that my father is going away—"

"The general going to leave Paris?"

" Oh! only for a few weeks. He is going to make a tour of inspection in the provinces. Meanwhile he sends me into the country, to my aunt de Louvercy, on the Eure, in the heart of the woods. My aunt is the best of women, but she lives alone in her château with her son, my cousin Roger, you know, who has been half mad since he was so frightfully wounded in the war; poor fellow! he has no longer a human figure—no arms, no legs! It is the greatest pity, you know, but—you can fancy what a household it is! So I said to my father, 'I will go, but it will be exile, despair, it will be death—at least unless you allow me to take Charlotte d'Erra with me!' 'Take Charlotte d'Erra,' said my father —and I take thee!"

" But, my dear little—"

" Ah! do not say no, I beg of you, or I shall expire at your feet! Make this sacrifice for me. Besides, who knows? we may not be so much bored, perhaps; we can wander off by ourselves, we can ride on horseback, we can play duets. And then, too, there are several neighbors about there; indeed, my dear, we shall turn their heads, you with your insolent beauty, I with my little—with whatever attractions there are which are peculiar to me, and which people commonly call ' canine.' "

I frowned and said, in my gravest contralto, " What do you mean, Cécile ? "

She leaned upon her elbows with an air of bravado, and, showing me her little pointed teeth, she repeated, " Canine ! "

" Who taught you that nonsense ? "

" My father ! " said she.

" I fancy your mother would scold your father if she were living."

She looked at me fixedly with her large, clear eyes, which filled with tears ; she kissed my hands, and resumed in a low, supplicating tone, " You will come, will you not ? "

" But, my darling, I cannot leave my grandmother."

" Your grandmother ! I am to take her also. I have thought of everything ; I have written to my aunt, and here is a pressing invitation, in her own handwriting, for your grandmother. Take me to her ! "

Two minutes after, Cécile precipitated herself into the *salon*, pushing the door open abruptly.

My grandmother, whom the least noise startles, sprang trembling to her feet. "Ah! good Heavens! there has been an accident! I am sure something has happened. Tell me at once; what is it? what is it?"

"It is a letter from my aunt de Louvercy, madame."

"Ah! poor Mme. de Louvercy! Poor woman! How is she? What trials she has had! And her poor son! Ah! poor souls! Well, what does she want of me?"

"If you will have the goodness to read, madame?"

My dear grandmother read the letter and assumed a thoughtful air; when she raised her eyes, she saw Cécile kneeling at her feet upon the carpet, her hands clasped, and her pretty, dimpled face upturned.

"Truly! do you see that?" said my grandmother. "Bless her little heart!"

"You will go, madame?" said Cécile.

"Really! my dear child," replied my grandmother, kissing her forehead, "I must say that as a general rule I greatly dislike these sudden moves;

I have a profound horror of them. But, in the first place this is a little holiday arranged between you and Charlotte; and, in the second, Mme. de Louvercy sends me such a pressing and affectionate appeal; she inspires in me besides so much compassion, poor woman! However, understand me well, so far as incommoding myself is concerned: I like to have time to seriously settle down for a while. To go to a place in order to come away again, to unpack my trunks just to repack them, without stopping to take breath: none of that for me! I certainly would not wish to impose myself upon your aunt, but let us see—how long is this invitation for?"

"For as long as you please, madame; six weeks —two months."

"Ah! very good! that is even too much!" said my grandmother.

In short, it was agreed that the Countess d'Erra and I should go in a fortnight, and join my friend Cécile, who started yesterday, at Louvercy. Ten days will hardly be enough for our preparations, which are considerable, as one can judge by this simple detail, that my grandmother will take with her her large folding screen, in order to guard against the currents of air, which must rage, she says, in an old château. I survey this astonishing packing with apparent tranquillity, dreaming secretly of belfries, of northern towers, of galleries full of ancestors and ghosts, and also of that poor mutilated and suffering being who doubtless mingles his complaints with the moanings of the wind in the long corridors. All this, alas! enchants me.

May 23d.

I received this morning a letter from Cécile, which presents the sojourn at Louvercy in new colors, less sombre but perhaps less attractive to me. Here it is, word for word:

"CHÂTEAU DE LOUVERCY, *May 27th.*"

"My dearest, you are going to shudder—it was all a plot! In whom can we trust henceforth? My father, my aunt, both so generally esteemed, whose lives up to this time have been so irreproachable, have united in a dark conspiracy against a weak child!

"It was Monday; at five o'clock in the evening, I arrive at the station (where, parenthetically, there is a blind man who plays the Marseillaise upon his flageolet; I tell you this, that you may stop at this station and not at any other). I arrive, then, at the station and fall into the arms of my aunt. 'My dear aunt!' 'My dear niece, how do you do?' We get into the carriage. Before we had exchanged four words, I felt some mystery in the air—embarrassment on the part of my aunt, mysterious language, covert allusions. There are several people at the château; they feared it would be too wearisome for me before the arrival of my friend Charlotte. 'Ah, my aunt, can you think so?' They have gathered a little circle of companions suitable to my age; two young women, relatives of the late M. de Louvercy, Mmes. de Sauves and de Chagres. 'Thank you, aunt.' Then their husbands—'Bravo, aunt!' And the two brothers of these ladies, very agreeable young men, remarkably agreeable—(aside uneasily) 'Ahem! ahem!' (aloud with indifference) 'Indeed, aunt?' 'And tell me, have you brought some pretty dresses?'—'Ordinary ones, aunt, I was so far from expecting to find any one with you!' —'At your age, my child, one should always be prepared!'

"Do you seize the situation, my child? Does the conspiracy dawn upon you? Can you see the picture spread out before you?

"At last we enter the grounds of the château; on one side there is a little lake, with swans floating upon its surface, and upon the banks stand Mmes. de Sauves and de Chagres, with their husbands and their 'remarkable' brothers, forming an interesting family group. I bow, I blush, I spring to the ground; I embrace Mmes. de Sauves and de Chagres, and I run quickly to change my dress, while the echo repeats behind me: 'She is charming! she is charming!'

"My suspicions, which were inordinately awakened from the first moment, were confirmed in the evening, the next day, and the day following. My aunt's sinister château is suddenly transformed; it is an abode of pleasure, an enchanted dwelling, the scene of delightful fêtes and chivalrous tournaments, with a vague odor of orange-blossoms in the by-ways. Walks in the morning, cavalcades in the afternoon, dances and charades in the evening. Personally I am spoiled, indulged, idolized. My tastes are consulted, my least desires are understood, divined, fulfilled, before I express them. There is a touching emulation. I secretly wish for a bouquet of camellias; behold it! A box of bonbons from Boissier's; behold it! A red parrot; behold the parrot! A gilded cage to put it in; behold the cage! The moon; behold the moon!

"You see, my dearest, how grave the circumstances are. There is no longer the shadow of a doubt. My perfidious aunt and my guilty father have resolved to marry me at once. There are two aspirants, between whom I am given a choice. Allow me to present them to you. Mmes. de Sauves and de Chagres have each a brother, and these two young men, who are cousins, bear the same family name, MM. René and Henri de Valnesse. Here I am reminded of the historical parallels in which you excelled at the convent (between Charles V. and Francis I. for example; do you remember? If one was the more skillful politician, the other was the greater warrior, etc.). To apply to MM. de Valnesse this figure of rhetoric, I will tell you that, if one is dark, the other is light; that if one finds eye-glasses necessary, the other makes use of a single glass; that one sings sentimental ballads

which make me weep, and the other comic songs
which make me laugh; that both look equally well
on foot and on horseback; that both are good
waltzers, agreeable in conversation, perfectly cultivated, possessed of equal fortunes, and both, if I
can believe certain appearances, equally disposed to
place these fortunes at the feet of the innocent person who writes these lines.

"You will ask, 'Is your choice made?' No,
my angel, my choice is not made. They please me
very nearly in the same degree; and, as I cannot
marry both, I await the wise Charlotte, that I may
take her advice and feel a preference. 'Thy choice
will be my choice, and thy God will be my God!'
Come, then, my dearest, without delay; for this
suspense is terrible, and you understand that there
would be little humanity in leaving the tenderest
of friends in so violent a situation.

"CÉCILE DE STÈLE.

"P. S.—All this time my poor cousin Roger remains sombre and savage in his tower, and goes out
only to run over the country in a *panier,* to which
he attaches the most vicious horses. My aunt pre-

tends that he chooses them expressly, and that he wishes to kill himself. Very sad, is it not? Farewell, dearest; come quickly."

This letter has troubled me very much. Cécile is almost a sister to me. Although we are of the same age, there has always been a slight maternal tinge in the affection I have felt for her. The great event which is preparing for her fills me with emotion; with joy, but also with anxiety. I wish so much that she may be happy! She so thoroughly deserves to be so, dear child! Her nature is so affectionate, so gracious, so sincere! Her head is a little giddy, perhaps, but her heart is sound and pure, always submissive, always prompt to repent. There is in her, as she likes to repeat, something of the angel and the demon, but particularly of the angel. This frivolous, impulsive, affectionate creature seems to me, more than most women, to need to be well married, well loved, and well guided.

I also greatly dread the responsibility that her loving confidence imposes upon me. I am very young and very inexperienced to direct the choice on which her destiny depends. At least I shall throw into it all my zeal and all my conscience. It seems to me that I shall be more exacting for her than I would be for myself even. MM. de Valnesse will do well to be on their guard. Behold, the archangel cometh with the flaming sword, who watches at the gate of paradise!

CHÂTEAU DE LOUVERCY, June 6th.

My dream is realized; there is a northern tower, and my room is actually in it! It is charming! But let us proceed in order. My grandmother and I arrived this afternoon. On getting out of the car, we saw at once the blind man and his flageolet; then Mme. de Louvercy and Cécile in an open landau; also, two cavaliers caracoling about in the little square before the station, calming by voice and hand their horses, which the whistle of the locomotive had frightened. By a furtive glance from Cécile, I recognized the two aspirants to her hand, and I made a curious inspection of their persons, while they apparently paid me the same compliment. My first impression was favorable. The two faces are reassuring, gay, and frank—the faces of honest men. My heart is easier on that score.

We rolled along over the white road, in the midst of a cloud of dust, with a cavalier at each door of the carriage as escort. Normandy apple-trees, with their clusters of pink blossoms, lined the way on the right and left. The sky was of a delicate, opaline blue. Cécile, in a toilet of the color of the heavens, fairly beamed with pleasure, pressed my hands, and threw a smile, now on this side, now on that, to maintain a balance, and we were happy. How good it is to live sometimes!

I had not seen Mme. de Louvercy for several years. She has grown astonishingly old. Her hair is quite white, forming a marvelous frame for her beautiful, sad face. Under her eyes she has two bluish furrows, which have certainly been caused by tears. She speaks little of her griefs, and generally only by allusion. On the way to the château I heard her telling my grandmother how the unfortunate condition of her son had absorbed her entirely for a long time; but that she ought to have remembered that Cécile had no longer a mother, and that she had a duty toward her also to perform. All this was said in a tone of extreme reserve, without dwelling upon it, and with a smile of kindly

welcome, very touching on this background of in-
consolable sadness. The poor woman is so much
the more to be pitied as her son was charming, they
say, before he met with this horrible wound, which
has mutilated, crippled, and disfigured him.

The noise of the wheels is suddenly muffled upon
the turf and moss; we enter the avenue under a
leafy arch, at the end of which I see the elegant
and severe façade of the château, in the Renaissance
style I believe. Here is the court, which is at the
same time a flourishing garden; there the swans
which beat their wings at our approach; Mmes. de
Sauves and de Chagres, who wave their handker-
chiefs on the veranda, while their husbands throw
away their cigars and wave their hats. It is a tri-
umph! They are very goodly to look upon, these
two young families, and they promise well.

A moment after, my grandmother and I are in-
stalled in our apartment by Cécile. While I brush
off the dust of travel, she interrogates me feverish-
ly: "Well! Tell me quickly, at a glance, how do
they strike you?"

"I like them very much; they are very charming."

2

" Truly ?—let me embrace you! but which do you prefer—tell me quickly, the blonde or the brunette, M. René or M. Henri ? "

" So far I prefer neither the one nor the other; and you, little one— "

" Did I not write you that I should wait for you before I could feel a preference ? You are to tell me which you prefer, and I will accept him."

" I assure you, Cécile, your confidence appalls me."

" Listen. I am going to put you between the two gentlemen at dinner; you are to study them, to sound them thoroughly, do you understand ? I will tell you what I want to know, and upon what you are to examine them particularly, and after dinner you are to render me a strict account of the result. Well, now, I desire to know first which of the two has the more true and enduring affection for me; then—and this is very important—which has the better character; then, which is the more intelligent and cultivated, for I desire a husband who will do me honor ; then, which has the more generous and charitable soul—I think much of this detail; then, which is fonder of travel, for I consider that important also; then which—do not laugh, Charlotte, it is very serious ! "

"I laugh, Cécile, because you really ask too much for a single sitting. Still I will bend all my energies to it. I will do my best."

Cécile leaves me with my maid, and I prepare myself for dinner. I put on a very simple dress, the modest toilet of a confidante ; dark colors, square-necked waist, lace, and a red rose in my hair, *à l'Espagnole.* I am not a fright, and that suffices.

Before the second bell sounds, I have time enough left to examine my apartment. It surpasses my hopes. It might be the chamber of a captive princess, hung in grand, old, mysterious tapestries, and having deep-set windows, like a chapel. I am, as I have said, in the north tower ; this tower is a very high, square pavilion, with a feudal aspect, and of a much more ancient date than the rest of the château, of which it forms the right wing. It is especially dedicated to the use of M. Roger de Louvercy, who can more easily satisfy his taste for solitude and isolation there. They even raised, a while ago, a transverse trellis, disguised as a palisade, which serves as a barrier, so to speak, between the château and the tower, and which enables this unfortunate young man to live completely by himself, when it suits him, as is always the case when his mother is not alone, for he has taken an unhappy fancy that to everybody but his mother he is an object of horror and disgust. Several buildings, recently constructed, form his special court, where he has his stables and kennels, and which has an egress into the open country. He can thus go and come without crossing the principal court.

M. Roger occupies the apartments upon the ground-floor, while my grandmother and I are on the first story. We were admitted into this sacred place, as Cécile says, as being the most quiet of the guests. We are, besides, in communication with the château by corridors on each story, and can move about freely without the fear of meeting M. de Louvercy. Cécile, however, has warned us that he sometimes goes up to the second story to write in his library; "But," added she, "nothing will be easier for you than to avoid him, poor boy! You will hear his crutch on the staircase."

Notwithstanding this safeguard, I confess I se-

cretly promised myself to take the first opportunity
to look at this sombre deformity; my curiosity has
just this moment been satisfied, and at the same
time punished, for my sympathetic compassion for
his great misfortune can hardly survive the shock
of what I have seen and heard. The window of
my dressing-room opens upon the little court, where
the stables reserved for the special use of M. de
Louvercy are. I had just fastened the red rose in
my lace, when this court suddenly resounded with a
confused tumult of trampling, barking, calling, impatient clamor, and, I must say, of frightful swear-
ing. I drew aside the curtain lightly, and I saw,
first, two enormous Newfoundland dogs jumping at
the nose of a horse, which was all white with sweat
and foam; then, a kind of basket dog-cart, and in
it M. de Louvercy, very easily recognizable by his
mutilated arm and leg. As for his face, I could
distinguish only two long blonde mustaches, drawn
down *à la Tartare*. M. de Louvercy was calling in
a furious tone two servants, who doubtless did not
expect him so soon, and who were running like mad.
He greeted them with a volley of savage words,
during which they assisted him to descend from the

carriage. I had quickly drawn the curtain, and saw no more. I was overcome; this shocking sight destroys for me all the effect produced by his misfortune. My dear neighbor, we shall hardly be very neighborly!

At last we are at table. Cécile has placed me, according to her programme, between the two young rivals. I have M. de Valnesse the brunette on my right, and on my left M. de Valnesse the blonde; an arrangement, by-the-way, which seems to astonish Mme. de Louvercy much. Cécile sits opposite us, in order to better watch my operations. She is beside the curé of Louvercy, whom she endeavors to make laugh when he drinks. She laughs heartily herself, at the same time warning me with her eyes to do my duty. She evidently thinks that I am showing a little weakness. The truth is, I am meeting with unforeseen difficulties; MM. de Valnesse are both very polite, but they do not lend themselves to my investigation; they hardly reply to me; something seems to paralyze them; they look at me with a sort of uneasy stupor; they appear much preoccupied with the red rose in my hair. But that is not the point, my dear friends.

We were hardly out of the dining-room when Cécile took me aside. "Well! what have you discovered?"

"I have discovered that they are timid; that is something already."

"Timid!" echoed Cécile, "because you do not encourage them enough. You must encourage them if you want them to become familiar and gain confidence."

That appeared reasonable to me. I did encourage them gently, and, in fact, with the aid of the coffee, I found them becoming pliable, little by little. They both sang for me. Both asked me to waltz repeatedly, and after each waltz I kept them a moment for a chat. Meanwhile Cécile wandered about in the strangest fashion, now bursting into causeless laughter, now tossing the music about on the piano; suddenly she disappeared, and, fearing that she was not well, I went after her.

I found her in the court of the château in the dusk of the twilight; she was walking very rapidly, like some one taking exercise after a bath. When I approached, she pretended not to see me, and

continued her walk, turning her back upon me.
I called her: "Cécile!"

"What?"

"Are you suffering?"

"No."

"Well! what is the matter?"

"Nothing!"

I looked in her face, and she repeated: "No,
nothing! nothing, at least, that I ought not to have
foreseen, if I had had the least sense. As soon as
you arrive with your goddess-like face, it stands to
reason that I am overlooked! Oh! of course it is
not your fault that you were made like that; I
reproach you with nothing: that is to say, begging
your pardon, you could dispense with coquetry, my
dear. When a woman is as beautiful as you are,
and a coquette into the bargain, then good-by!
nothing more is possible."

"Truly, Cécile, I do not know whether to laugh
or be angry. What does this mean? You beg me,
you beseech me, you supplicate me, to study these
two young men—"

"Well, you study 'these two young men' too
much, and they study you too much!"

"Indeed! Do you wish me to return, then?"

She seized my hands. "Oh! no!" and after a pause, becoming tender, "I am stupid, am I not?" She threw her head on my breast and burst into tears. I quieted her as one would a child, and she suddenly resumed all her vivacity and habitual tenderness. "Listen—I have a superb idea: you will choose for yourself the one who pleases you most, and I will take the other. We will be cousins, almost sisters; it will be delicious! Besides, it is right that you should choose before me, you are my superior in every respect! It is quite right! quite right!"

"Dearest, you are the best little soul in the world, but I cannot accept your arrangement. And be sure of this: MM. de Valnesse are, and always will be, to me only the aspirants to your hand; this title gives them in my eyes an absolutely sacred character, and forbids any personal pretension even in thought. It seems to me it would be a gross offense to both delicacy and friendship. Do you believe me? Are you reassured?"

"I believe you. I adore you! Come and continue your studies."

We returned to the drawing-room, where I continued my studies, but more moderately, since zeal
has its dangers.

The old belfry-bell sounds—with what a charm
in the night and in the woods!

Great Heavens! two o'clock in the morning!
Are you not ashamed, mademoiselle?

June 12th.

Is movement synonymous with pleasure, and is
it enough to be stirring to be amused? If this is
so, then I am too much amused. "What shall we
do this morning? What shall we do this afternoon?
What shall we do this evening?" This is the re-
frain of the house; and behold us setting out on
foot, on horseback, in the carriage, regardless of
everything, full of life! A spirit of laughter ac-
companies us, returns with us, sits at table, dances
and sings with us, and does not leave us even in the
halls.

This morning early I wished to refresh myself
by a solitary walk in the park. I descended from
my tower with cat-like step, and when I had reached
the middle of the staircase I suddenly heard the

sharp sound of a crutch on the steps below, warning me of the approach of M. de Louvercy, who was apparently on the way to his library. I held my breath for a moment. I was about to bravely turn my back and take refuge in my room, but there was no longer time. We were face to face, M. Roger and I. Suddenly perceiving me, he became pale, as if he had seen a ghost. He made an embarrassed gesture as if to bow, and in his confusion he let fall his unfortunate crutch; it rolled down the staircase. I cannot describe the expression of profound distress depicted upon his face: it was a mixture of grief, humiliation, and anger. He held the baluster firmly with his right hand, while his mutilated left arm and shortened leg remained in air, without support. I hastily descended the steps, and picked up the crutch, returned quickly, and replaced it under his arm. He fixed his dark-blue eyes upon me, and said, in a low, grave voice, " I thank you ! " Then he continued his way and I mine.

This little scene has restored my interest in him. In the first place, I knew he made a tremendous effort to spare me a volley of the soldier-like imprecations of which he appears so prodigal. Then,

too, in spite of the involuntary antipathy with
which deformed beings generally inspire me, I am
far from finding him so repulsive as Cécile had described him.   He is one-armed, and one leg is shortened and seemingly paralyzed ; but his face is hand-
some and refined, and the slight scar on his forehead
does not disfigure him.   He has, perhaps, a shy and
bewildered air, which is particularly noticeable on
account of the careless state of his hair, and his long,
too long mustaches.

I was entering the park, when Cécile perceived
me from her window ; three minutes after, she was
trampling down the grass by my side, hopping along
like a bird.   I told her of my meeting with her
cousin.

"Ah, good gracious ! how he must have sworn ! "

"Not at all."

"You astonish me !   The fact is, he is in good-
humor to-day ; he expects his friend this evening."

"What friend ? "

"The Commandant d'Éblis, don't you know ? "

"No, I do not know—who is he ? "

"I thought I had told you ; it was he who saved
Roger's life at Coulmiers.   They had been very in-

timate for years—since St. Cyr. The moment Roger
was struck by that bomb, M. d'Éblis carried him
away in his arms like a child, in the midst of the
firing and under the feet of the horses. It was glorious! And since that time he has never ceased to
be perfect in Roger's eyes. He even found means
to attach him to life by inducing him to write the
history of this frightful war. They are both occupied with it. M. d'Éblis comes to see him often;
he brings him all the documents which may be useful for his work. He is himself very highly cultivated, very learned—a cavalry chief of staff at thirty
years; that is doing well!"

"But tell me, dearest, will not this fascinating
person prove a third thief?"

"M. d'Éblis!" exclaimed Cécile. "Great Heavens! my dear, I would as soon marry Croquemi-
taine himself. He is severe! he is terrible! I like
him well enough, however, on account of his conduct toward Roger. But we have hardly met more
than two or three times. He seems to look upon
me as a baby, and I regard him as a father. But,
seriously, Charlotte, do you not think it time to decide between MM. de Valnesse?"

"There is no great haste, it seems to me."

"I beg your pardon!"

"Your position between these two gentlemen has nothing disagreeable in it."

"Truly? You think so? and my heart, my weak heart, what do you think of that?"

"Has it spoken?"

"No, but it is impatient to speak; it burns to speak! Only give it the word!"

Seeing that she really did not desire a change, I replied by some pleasantry or other, and we entered the château, whither the breakfast-bell summoned us.

The truth is, the choice between the two candidates seems to me very difficult. The result of my observations in regard to them continues to be satisfactory and embarrassing : satisfactory, because they are both endowed with the most admirable qualities; embarrassing, because these qualities seem to me so nearly equal in both. They have the same kind of wit; in their types of character and their personal physique the points of resemblance can only be explained by their near relationship. In fact, I believe they are both the best of their kind.

They are two good fellows, who have refined tastes and pleasing talents, of ordinary intelligence, but honest and with great delicacy of feeling. They bear their rivalry and their mutual pretensions with a chivalrous courtesy which is very pleasing.

The trouble is, that I love Cécile so much that I could wish for her an absolutely perfect husband, an exception, something unique. But would it be wise to pursue an ideal, which perhaps does not exist, when something almost as rare, and which one may never meet again, is close at hand? A man of superior intellect has almost always, so far as my experience goes, faults of character equal to his abilities, and in proportion to his achievements. Are there not in reality more chances of happiness in this honest mediocrity that MM. de Valnesse represent with so much grace and distinction?

My "uneasy conscience" is tortured by these great questions which interest so dear a destiny. But, upon my word, I admire the singular tranquillity of mind with which Cécile, whatever she may say, awaits my decision, in order to pronounce hers. For my part, I have certainly never found myself in a similar position; but I am sure I should feel less

serenity and more personal determination. However, that remains to be seen!

Same day, Midnight.

This evening has been less noisy and less frivolous than the preceding. The presence of the Commandant d'Éblis has thrown cold water over us all,
Cécile says. In my opinion it has simply raised the
ordinary range of our little circle a trifle. I have
often noticed the strange influence which a truly
distinguished man exercises in society. He gives,
involuntarily and unwittingly, a new soul to things.
Whether he speaks or is silent, it matters little ; it
is enough that he is there. All are raised more or
less to his level, and seem to live more fully. He
establishes a more active current and a superior
plane of intercourse. The slightest incidents ac-
quire interest, and the diversions have at once more
moderation and more savor. One is untiringly alert
and yet at ease while he is present. One is often
glad to see him go, yet regrets his departure and
feels smaller in his absence. It is easy to see that
less importance is attached to what is said, because
he is no longer there to hear; also to what is done,
because he does not know of it.

This afternoon, M. de Louvercy went to the station with his *panier* to meet the Commandant d'Éblis ; when they entered into the little court before the stables, I found myself, partly by chance and partly by curiosity, at the window of my dressing-room. I drew my curtain aside : M. d'Éblis had just jumped from the *panier*, and was holding his arms out laughingly to M. de Louvercy, who, laughing also, slid to the earth on the breast of his friend. There was, it seemed to me, such a touching likeness to the terrible scene at Coulmiers, and I tried to fancy the violent emotions of battle and the fever of heroism on the two faces, now so smiling and tranquil.

M. d'Éblis dined with us. He is a man of medium height and rather stiff appearance, with that grave and correct elegance which characterizes officers in civil life. It must be allowed that, at a first glance, there seems to be something extremely severe and even hard in his expression; fine, cold features, sallow complexion, thick mustaches, very black and calm eyes—these are what strike one at first, and these are not very reassuring. But the slightest smile which appears gives an air of good-

ness to it all, that invites confidence at once.   One
takes courage as soon as he speaks, for his voice is
singularly sweet and musical.   There is a charm ...
simply listening to this music, coming from those
frightful mustaches.

I had this pleasure several times during dinner,
having been placed at table near M. d'Éblis.   We
began with silence; I was timid, and perhaps at
heart he was no braver than I; for, although he
has a severe expression, I have my own, too, of that
sort, and I have often remarked that I excite
timidity at first.   Then very suddenly, breaking
the ice, "Mademoiselle," he said to me, "I have
heard you talked of a good deal to-day."

"Indeed, monsieur?"

"I have learned that you are compassionate toward the unhappy."

"Monsieur!"

"You were kind to my poor friend Roger this
morning; I know that."

"Any one in the world in my place, I am sure,
would have done as I did."

"Doubtless 'any one in the world' would give
alms; but it was the manner."

I told him that I was flattered by his compliment, for he ought to be a judge of good actions,
᾿ᵗⁿᶜ he had certainly been more useful to M. Roger
ι I had been, and than I could ever have an opportunity of being.

He bowed, and answered in a low, sad tone, " I
am not sure that I rendered him a service—in bringing him out of that ! "

We rose from the table, and still continued the
conversation, discovering each other's likes and dis-
likes on all topics, particularly upon the subject of
Wagner's music, which he liked and I did not.

A saucy prank of Cécile caused an unwelcome
interruption. Cécile, who had been entirely occupied in making her curé laugh while he was drinking, was suddenly seized with the idea of riding a
couple of cherries, joined by their stems, jockey-
wise on her nose, holding up her pretty chin to
preserve their balance. Every one laughed, and
MM. de Valnesse applauded heartily. Then, calling a servant to her, she broke the cherries apart,
and, placing each on a plate, said, " Take that plate
to M. Henri de Valnesse and this to M. René."

While the young gentlemen gallantly placed the

cherries in the button-holes of their coats, the Commandant d'Éblis watched the proceeding with wide-open eyes. Cécile noticed him and exclaimed, with her ingenuous audacity, " You seem astonished, commandant ? "

" Not at all, mademoiselle."

" Pardon me, you seem very much astonished. Be frank; my little jest appears to you in very bad taste, does it not ? "

" Mademoiselle, everything that you do appears to me charming."

" No ; you are right : it was in very bad taste, but I will explain my character to you. It is very complicated, in some sense contradictory ; and you will understand why : it is because there are within me an angel and a demon."

" In that respect, mademoiselle," said M. d'Éblis, "you have many companions. We all have an angel that we try, more or less, to listen to, and a demon that we try, more or less, to silence. However, the demon that suggested to you to put the cherries on your nose cannot be a very wicked demon."

" Thank you, commandant," answered Cécile ;

"the lesson is there, but it is a kindly one. As I said this morning to your charming neighbor, you are a father to me."

M. d'Éblis bowed with a smile, and we resumed our *tête-à-tête.* If I can trust certain indications, this valiant soldier must be, as old epitaphs say, as good a son as he is a friend. He has a grave and tender way of saying, "My mother," which seems to me a revelation. The word is constantly on his lips. "For my mother's sake;" "my mother wishes it;" "it pleases my mother." In a moment of abstraction he even let fall the word "mamma!" He reddened slightly under his tan and recalled himself; but that childish appellation, in that gentle tone, from this vigorous man, was not without charm.

After dinner, Cécile came with her unequaled grace to offer her hand to the commandant and sign a truce with him. They talked together some time in a corner, looking toward me at intervals, so that I knew they were speaking of me. Cécile, in passing, whispered to me, "My dear, you have made havoc in the 'staff.'"

I have no desire to create havoc; but, if this

means that I am in sympathy with him, I confess quite plainly that I am very much pleased.

A moment after I was asked to sing something. I have a *mezzo-soprano* voice, quite strong, and well cultivated, but I am not fond of exhibiting it in public ; my reluctance is well known, and I am generally left in quiet. However, I went to the piano and began the air from " Norma "—" Casta Diva." My surprise was keen, and my mortification not less so, when, after singing the first few bars, I saw the Commandant d'Éblis softly open the door of the *salon* and disappear. I felt that my performance was mediocre ; but I did not on that account cease singing with the conscientious care that I bring to everything I do. I had just finished in the midst of a flattering murmur, when M. d'Éblis reëntered and came toward me.

" Mademoiselle," said he, pointing to a window that had been opened on account of the heat of the evening, " Roger is out there on the bench in the court. He would be infinitely obliged to you if you would repeat the air from ' Norma.' " " Willingly," I replied, and I sang the air over again with all my heart.

I was well repaid for my trouble. Mme. de Louvercy, who, during the singing had remained perfectly radiant by the window, leaned out of it the moment I left the piano, and exchanged a few words with her son. Then she came toward me, took my hands, and, kissing me, said with emotion: "Thank you for him and for myself; it is the first time in a long while that I have sean a gleam of happiness in his eyes." Truly, it was a success to have brought the savage out of his den. I am proud of it, and thereupon I am going to sleep a happy woman.

June 25th.

I have not written for eight or ten days. I have been seized by my old scruples; I feared to give a body to my fancies in fixing them on these pages; I was afraid of strengthening impressions which it may be wiser to let dissolve in air. Again it is my grandmother who quite unconsciously encourages me to follow my fatal inclination, and to continue my confidential relations with my locked diary and myself.

When I entered her room this morning to wish

her good-day, she embraced me more tenderly than
usual, and, taking one of my hands in hers, said,
" Have you nothing to tell me, my child ? "

" I think so, grandmamma."

" Ah ! M. d'Éblis is making love to you, is he
not ? "

" I do not know whether M. d'Éblis is making
love to me or not, dear grandmamma, for he has
never said a word distantly resembling a declaration.
But he seems to like to be with me ; he speaks
to me with a kind of respect, of confidence, and at
the same time of timidity even, that I do not find
in every one. He addresses all that he says to
me personally, and the least thing that I say he
treasures as if all my words were pearls. If that
can be called ' making love ' to a woman, I really
believe that he is making love to me a little."

" I have noticed it," said my grandmother, grave-
ly ; " and it does not displease you ? "

" No."

" No, naturally ; but the mischief is not done
yet, is it ? You are not in love with this gentleman ? "

" In love ?—no."

" He simply pleases you ? "

" A little."

" Yes, and he does me also. Listen to me, my
dear child : we did not come here to find a husband,
but, if we do find one, we may as well take him here
as elsewhere, may we not ? Only, you know, my
dear little one, that an affair of this kind is very
serious, and it is well to think twice. For my part,
after I caught a glimpse of the attractions of this
man, I did not wait three minutes to gather information from Mme. de Louvercy ; still further, I have
written to Paris. I am informed from all sides.
Well, these investigations all show that there are no
grave objections to him. On the contrary ! But
still, dear child, you know that neither my opinion
nor that of others ought to influence your personal
feelings ; there are no serious objections, that is all ;
family, reputation, fortune even, are all very good,
very suitable. But, in spite of all that, I conjure
you, dear, do not yield too quickly, too lightly to
your first impression ; take time to let it deepen. I
know you so well, my child ; you would be so utterly
miserable if you were not happy. You are one of
those who do not love twice, and it is necessary for

3

such not to deceive themselves. When you have
opened your heart to a tender sentiment—when
Love, to speak plainly, has entered there, he will remain; he will seat himself as upon a royal throne,
that he will leave only with life."

The angel that is within me, as Cécile says, had
long ago softly murmured, although in terms less
kindly, the truths that I heard aloud from my
grandmother. It had put me on my guard; it had
warned me that my first would be my only love,
all-powerful, eternal, and that I must choose well
or die.

These may be only phrases; but I believe them.
To love a man who merits all my affection, all my
esteem, all my respect, and to be loved by him—
that is my dream! Am I truly, truly, near its ful-
fillment? Let me reflect. That a man like M.
d'Éblis, of an agreeable and at the same time im-
pressive exterior, of unexceptionable manners, of
unusual merit, of a character at once heroic and
tender—that a man so formed and almost perfect
should satisfy all the desires of a woman's heart,
nothing, alas! is more natural. That a young girl
who feels or fancies herself honored by the particu-

lar attentions of this distinguished person should be flattered and touched by them, that she should find a peculiar pleasure in her daily relations with this superior intelligence and this charming spirit, that she should experience a secret intoxication in the thought of changing this intimacy of a few days into an eternal union—nothing can be more simple and, still, more natural.

But what seems to me less natural and more doubtful is that a man like M. d'Éblis, who, it seems to me, can choose at his pleasure from all the world a companion worthy of him, should seriously attach himself in so short a time to the pale and romantic Charlotte. One so easily believes what one desires! Am I not deluding myself? Am I not deceived by a few superficial courtesies which are addressed to me as they might be to any one? One is in the country, one is bored, one sees Cécile entirely monopolized and engrossed while I am left alone; one finds this a little unjust, and shows me a few attentions out of humanity. Is not that it? Still he is incapable, unless I am greatly deceived, of disturbing a woman's peace. But how could I ever have pleased him? By what merits? If I have any he cannot know them. I do not reveal myself easily; I do not tell my secrets. I say nothing to him beyond what I ought to say—mere conventionalities. I know very well that I am pretty enough, and at first sight that is undoubtedly an attraction, even to a man like him. But if there be nothing but that, how many women more beautiful than I has he not met in his life?

Thinking the matter well over, I feel that my principal virtue in his eyes, and that which gains me his sympathy, is my obliging compassion for his poor friend Roger. Evidently his friendship for M. de Louvercy is a ruling passion with him, and he would be apt to like any one who flatters it. On the day of his arrival, I had, without at all intending it, ministered to this weakness, and since then, now that I think of it, I have had frequent opportunities of touching this fine point in his heart. It is now several days since M. Roger, thanks to M. d'Éblis's affectionate influence, became our habitual companion at table. The first time that he consented to take his place among us, at the solicitation of the commandant, the astonishment was great and the rejoicings also, especially his mother's. The poor lady fairly beamed. He had had his hair cut, and his toilet, which is usually very much neglected, was carefully arranged. His fine face, pale and stern at first, gradually lighted up and softened in our company, although it clouded and contracted again whenever the slightest incident recalled his infirmity, for instance when he had to accept assistance at the table, or in sitting down and rising. It is in these little things that I am able to show him the real pity that he inspires in me. After dinner he is accustomed to sit a few minutes on one of the garden-benches, which are placed under the windows of the ground-floor. The other evening Cécile and I, seeing him ill at ease on the bench, made a signal to each other; Cécile went after a pile of cushions in the *salon*, which she passed through the window to me; M. d'Éblis, to whom I delivered them one by one, attempted to arrange them as a support for the wounded arm and leg. But he went about it very awkwardly, and so, scolding him laughingly for his clumsiness, and saying to M. de Louvercy, "Permit me, monsieur," I adjusted the cushions with a woman's superior tact. As M. de Louvercy thanked me a trifle constrainedly, M. d'Éblis said to him, gayly, "What a good hospital nurse, isn't she, Roger ?"

M. d'Éblis seems to me more grateful for these little attentions than he who is the direct object of them. He looks at me at such times in a searching, thoughtful, and, I believe, almost tender way. However, the feeling which he may have for me betrays itself only by these slight impulses of gratitude, and by the kind of pleasure that he seems to find in my company and my conversation.

"Can I find enough here to make it wise for me to open my heart, to nourish a preference which doubtless is still but a passing dream, but which, if I abandon myself to it, will become to-morrow, perhaps, a profound passion ?

July 5th.

This morning, after an almost sleepless night, I rose at daybreak, that is to say, at seven o'clock, and I resolved to do an unusual thing. I put my beloved locked diary under my arm; and taking my umbrella in one hand and my bamboo case, which contains all the necessary materials for writing, in the other, I softly left the north tower by the south

door. Opposite this door is a broad avenue; in
this avenue there is on the left hand a winding
path; at the end of this path there is a thicket,
and in this thicket a statue of Flora, or Ceres, or
Pomona, with a rustic table and three chairs. It is
a charming spot, especially on a lovely summer
morning like this. A kind of religious twilight
always reigns here; the leaves fall together and in-
terlace in a sort of lattice-work, through which one
gets glimpses of blue sky. The sun throws here
and there on the ground, on the chairs, on the
shoulders of the goddess, luminous bands, rays
which seem sifted through the stained glass of a
church. A slight odor of the orange-tree mingles
with the perfume of the rose and of the white aca-
cia-fruit; and, to complete the picture, one hears
from an unseen ravine the musical murmur of a little brook, the home of the swans, which passes by
here, one knows not how.

One knows no more why the thought occurred
to Charlotte d'Erra to choose this charming spot in
which to write the recital of yesterday evening.
Perhaps she wished to frame richly, in gold and
flowers, a simple episode in the life of a young girl,

which may become—if God in his goodness should permit—the first page in the life of a woman.

Yesterday, after dinner, we were distributed, according to our daily custom, about the court of the château, to breathe the fresh evening air, mingled with the perfume of roses and of cigars. M. de Louvercy smoked, and stretched himself on his favorite bench that we had piled up with cushions. Cécile, always as restless as a star, was suddenly seized with the unlucky notion of playing with her cousin's crutch. She examined it at first timidly, then she became better acquainted with it, and used it to practise an apprenticeship as a huntress, her father having sent her a few days before a little gun with which she proposed to destroy all the rabbits and squirrels in the park. Meanwhile she exercised herself with the crutch in " shoulder arms," " carry arms," and then took aim at imaginary rabbits represented by MM. Henri and René de Valnesse. I saw M. Roger frown painfully, and the Commandant d'Éblis bite his mustache; I gave Cécile a severe look, but I lost my trouble. Encouraged by the expansive appreciation of her two admirers, she aggravated her thoughtlessness cruelly by placing the crutch under her arm, and trying to walk with one foot in the air, like her poor disabled cousin. She took a few steps in the court in this way with great gravity, and without a shadow of malice, simply to see, she said, if it were very inconvenient. M. Roger pretended to smile, but his brow was dark with anger. I perceived it, and would have gone to Cécile to warn her, but M. d'Éblis anticipated me. He stepped up to her quickly, and whispered to her with energy a few words that I did not hear. But I heard perfectly Cécile reply to him, " Always lessons ! " " This one is well merited, I think," said M. d'Éblis. She seemed moved, and she hesitated a moment between her demon and her angel. Then she took a few precipitate steps toward the house, and gently placed the crutch against the bench ; and, detaching from the trellis which surrounded the window a branch of jasmine, she tried to place it in M. de Louvercy's button-hole, saying to him, " I will decorate you, cousin ! "

M. Roger seized the flower from her hands and threw it on the gravel. " You are a fool ! " said he. He rose at the same time, and, bowing slightly to me, he went to his room.

As soon as he had disappeared, Cécile clasped
her hands and raised her shoulders. "There are
moments when I could kill myself!" cried she; at
the same time she let herself sink upon the bench
and hid her head in her hands, and we heard her
sob. M. d'Éblis exchanged a look of intelligence
and a smile with me; then, turning toward Cécile,
"Mademoiselle," said he, "your despair is excessive! For so small an offense, a childish indiscretion"—and, picking up the branch of jasmine, he
added, "Would you like to have me take your
flower to him?" Still weeping, she made a sign
that she would like it very much; then she raised
her head a little, and, smiling at M. d'Éblis through
her tears, "Always a father to me!" she exclaimed.

Then we walked off a little way to allow her to
recover herself. All Mme. de Louvercy's guests
were walking here and there in groups, talking in
low tones as if penetrated by the beauty of the
evening. It was serene and superb. A full moon
filled the vast court with its limpid splendor; there
was a silver sheen upon the water of the lake, in
the midst of which two large swans slept immovable in their snowy whiteness. Exchanging a few

indifferent words, M. d'Éblis and I walked back
and forth between the lake and the first trees of the
avenue, whose arched nave, in the midst of all this
brightness, remained sombre as a cathedral at midnight. After a silence, I said, " A scene so sweet
and peaceful must form a singular contrast to your
memories of the war, does it not, commandant ? "

He started. " Have you the gift of second-
sight, mademoiselle ? "

" I have scarcely the gift of first sight," said I,
laughingly, " for I am very near-sighted. But why
do you ask, monsieur ? "

" Because at that very moment my thoughts did
carry me back to a scene in my military life, to an
evening like this, but less tender although as peaceful."

" May I hear it ? "

He hesitated, sighed, then bowing slightly,
" Certainly. I was under Metz. On the evening
of which I speak, the 27th of October, I had been
detailed to carry some orders whose meaning did
not appear very clear to me. I was, in particular,
to arrest the march of one of our regiments, whose
number I have forgotten. I fulfilled my mission,

and was ready to return, waiting only to breathe
my horse a little. We were then in a plain near
a village called Colombey, I think; the terrible
tempests which marked those evil days were allayed
for a few hours; a tranquil moon was reflected in
the small pools which covered the country. The
imagination creates strange associations. There is
certainly little in the smiling loveliness which surrounds us here to remind one of those desolate
marshes; however, the moonlight on the water recalled them to me just now, and those beautiful
swans which are sleeping there remind me of my
escort of dragoons, immovable as they in their white
mantles. The regiment, while waiting new orders,
kept ranks, and rested on their arms. A large
bivouac-fire had been lighted, around which a few
officers conversed mournfully in low tones. The
rumor of a capitulation had circulated through the
camp since the evening before. The colonel, who
was a middle-aged man, with a grizzled mustache,
paced back and forth alone some distance away,
crushing in his hand the order that I had brought
him. Suddenly he approached me, and, seizing my
arm, ' Captain,' said he, in the tone of a man about

to mortally provoke another, 'two words, I pray you. You come from headquarters, you must know of it long before I. This is the end, is it not?'

"'They say so, colonel, and I believe it.'

"'You believe it! How can you believe such a thing?'

"He loosed my arm with a sort of violence, took a few steps, and, turning abruptly to me again, he fixed his eyes upon mine.

"'Prisoners, then?'

"'I fear so, colonel.'

"Again he was silent. He remained some time before me in an attitude of profound reflection, then, raising his head, he resumed, with unusual emotion in his voice:

"'And the colors?'

"'I do not know, colonel.'

"'Ah! you do not know?'

"He left me again, and recommenced his solitary walk for five or six minutes; then, advancing to the front of the men, he said, in a tone of command, 'The flag!'

"The standard-bearer stepped out of the ranks. The colonel seized the staff with one hand, and, raising the other toward the group of drummers, 'Beat to orders!' he said.

"The drums beat. The colonel approached the fire, carrying the flag raised high above him. He planted the staff on the ground, threw an earnest look around the circle of officers, and uncovered his head. They all followed his example; the waiting troops kept a death-like silence. He then hesitated a moment; I saw his lips tremble, his eyes fixed themselves with an expression of anguish on the glorious fragment of torn silk—sad symbol of his country! At last he took his resolution. He bent his knee, and softly laid the eagle in the burning fire. A more vivid flame suddenly shot up, showing more clearly the pale countenances of the officers. Every one wept.

"'Break ranks!' said the colonel, and a second time the mournful roll of the drums resounded.

"He resumed his *képi*, and came toward me. 'Captain,' said he to me, in a firm voice, 'when you return, have no scruple—none—in recounting what you have seen. I salute you.'

"'Colonel,' said I, 'will you permit me to embrace you?'

" He drew me violently to his breast, and, holding me so tightly as almost to suffocate me, ' Ah !
my poor child!' he murmured—' my poor child!' ''

At this point in his recital, M. d'Éblis turned
away, and I heard a sort of sob. I could not help
reaching out my hand to him. He seemed astonished; he took it and pressed it warmly. " You
comprehend, then, all one suffers in such moments ? "

" Yes;" and, as I would have withdrawn my
hand, he gently retained it. " If anything in the
world," added he, " could make me forget, it would
be a moment like this." I did not answer, and he
released my hand. After a few steps in silence,
" Shall we return ? " said I.

" Yes, whenever you wish." And we returned.

Nothing more. But, on the part of a man so
reserved and so loyal, was it not a great deal—was
it not everything ? These words, when I recall
them to myself, when I reread them, seem to me
almost without significance; but his deep, tender,
penetrating tone—was it not that of a heart which
offers itself sacredly and devotedly ?

Truly I believe so; and, if I may judge by myself, such a moment, a moment when two souls touch each other in so close a union, suffices to join them forever on earth and in heaven. My God, I pray thee, grant that I may not deceive myself!

July 13th.

It is now some days since I have had the courage to resume my pen. I do not understand what is going on; I do not understand what evil genius has touched the château with his wand, and suddenly saddened all the spirits, soured all the natures, and changed all the hearts therein, excepting mine, alas!

The first symptoms of this revolution were manifested the very evening that left upon me so happy —and, I very much fear, so deceptive—an impression. When I rejoined Cécile under the windows of the *salon* after separating from M. d'Éblis, I thought that she was sulky, and I asked the reason. As usual, she had to be urged to tell me; but, as I insisted, she drew me beneath the lilacs, and declared to me, in a serious tone and (from her lips) one of extreme bitterness, that I was a false friend, that I completely neglected all her interests, that I

abused her confidence, and that I amused myself
in some way or other, while she remained in suspense between her two lovers, in a horribly painful
and even ludicrous position. I bowed my head to
this storm, acknowledging to myself that I had
somewhat merited these reproaches, and that for
some time I had been more effectually engrossed by
my own interests than by hers. I calmed her as
best I could, alleging the usual difficulty of making
a choice, and promising to have a decisive conversation with her very soon, when I would try to end
our mutual irresolution.

It seems that, at the same time, a much more
serious quarrel had broken out between the Commandant d'Éblis and M. de Louvercy. Over what?
no one could tell me. I only learned from Mme.
de Chagres that M. de Louvercy, who at first sought
his apartments after the little scene with Cécile, had
suddenly returned to the court; that he had ac-
costed M. d'Éblis the moment I left him, and had
entered into conversation with him under the
gloomy arch of the avenue. There they were heard
talking with great animation; Mme. de Chagres
told me that the voice of M. de Louvercy especially

evinced a kind of rage or of grief that was almost frenzy. They were afterward seen to cross the court in silence, M. d'Éblis sustaining M. de Louvercy, who seemed to walk with even more than his usual difficulty. A few minutes after, Mme. de Louvercy was sent for in haste, as her son was suffering from a nervous attack. After this occurrence he did not appear among us for two or three days.

M. d'Éblis on his side neglected us a great deal during the same interval: he either remained shut up all day with his friend, or he rambled over the fields in his company, and we met him only at meals. He was unusually sad and silent; his attitude toward me was embarrassed, his language of a coldness quite new and apparently assumed. If it were possible for me to imagine that there had been any question of me in his quarrel with M. Roger, and that the latter had slandered me to M. d'Éblis, truly I would believe it. But the supposition is evidently inadmissible. Whatever may have been the subject of their disagreement, no trace of it remains between them. Their friendly union seems even closer than before; one would say that it had been strengthened by some new tie. A shade of this is especially plain in M. Roger's manner: in his relations with M. d'Éblis he displays a curiously affectionate tenderness, as if he would be pardoned for something. It is clear that the wrong was on his side. But what wrong?

Mme. de Louvercy knows apparently, for she is more pensive than usual. From contagion, doubtless, my grandmother appears preoccupied, and MM. de Valnesse themselves, as well as their sisters, mope in their corners.

For myself, I do not grow dismal over what I feel. I soared in the heavens among the stars; my wings were suddenly clipped, and I fell heavily to the earth. That is all. I force myself to forget this radiant illusion of a moment; but I cannot, and I fear that I shall never be able to.

July 22d.

Did I not despair too hastily? It seems to me that after that sudden squall everything returned little by little to the accustomed order. M. d'Éblis had certainly experienced something very disagreeable, which at first overruled every other feeling in him, and the dominance of which he had shaken off with difficulty. But at last, little by little, he

chased away this cloud, and seems now to have re-
gained his original free play of mind. At the same
time, he has resumed his habits of friendly and
confidential conversation with me, although I always find in him, when he is near me, something
sad and constrained. I do not know exactly what.
Nevertheless, he has under his grave exterior a
depth of gayety which Cécile especially has the gift
of arousing. Her fantastic and charming character,
so honest and frolicsome, interests and diverts him;
he censures and yet delights in her caprices, and
the arch tricks, at once graceful and grotesque,
which she is so fond of.

Yesterday morning, for example, she had resolved to try her skill with her gun in the wood
which surrounds the park. We all accompanied
her, and M. d'Éblis, in his military capacity, was
requested to preside over this dangerous expedition.
The rabbits ran about in the woods like mice in a
granary. It is scarcely necessary to say that Cécile
did not kill a single one; but, by way of compensation, she ~~failed~~ to cripple MM. de Valnesse, who
hastened to climb the trees whenever she aimed her
gun.

As we were returning gayly from this fruitless campaign, following a hollow which skirts the wood, Cécile perceived in the very middle of the pathway and in front of the bars of a pasture one of those brown-stone pitchers which are used in milking. "Stop!" said she; "see that pitcher down there all by itself." Piqued at her non-success with the rabbits, she at once conceived the triumphant idea of revenging herself on this unhappy pitcher: she quickly raised her gun to her shoulder and drew the trigger. "Hit!" cried she. The pitcher was shattered in pieces, and a stream of milk flowed over the ground. At the same moment the milk-maid, whom we had not seen before, as she was occupied in putting up the bars, suddenly appeared in the road. She was a little peasant about twelve years old, with her pale blonde hair covered with a child's cap. When she perceived her pitcher's mishap, the poor little girl raised and dropped her arms with a movement of profound consternation; then, after a pause of dumb stupor, she burst into tears, and sobbed out that her mother would beat her.

"No! no! be comforted," cried Cécile, "I will

pay you for your milk." While speaking, she had
advanced quickly, and, noticing that the bottom of
the broken pitcher still contained quite a quantity
of milk, "How fortunate that is!" said she; "I am
as thirsty as a wolf." She bent down, carefully
raised the fragment of the pitcher to her lips, and
drank the milk eagerly; then she stopped a moment
to take breath, and seeing the look of admiration
with which we regarded her—for she was perfectly
charming with the broken pitcher in her hand—
showing all her dimples—

"A Greuze!" said she.

After which she resumed drinking. When her
thirst was appeased, there was some milk still left
in the vessel. "Who will have some?" asked she.
The dark M. de Valnesse eagerly seized the pitcher,
and moistened his lips.

"It is twenty francs!" said Cécile.

The young man smilingly took out his purse,
and gave her a louis. M. de Valnesse, the blonde,
drank in his turn.

"Twenty francs!" repeated Cécile.—"It is your
turn, commandant!" she said then to M. d'Éblis,
who was greatly astonished.

" I, mademoiselle," said he—" I do not like milk, but here are my twenty francs."

Cécile placed the three louis in the hand of the little blonde milkmaid. " There," said she, " do not cry any more, my child!" and she kissed her heartily on both cheeks.

We continued our walk. Cécile was a little gloomy; at the end of a few steps: " Monsieur," said she to the Commandant d'Éblis, "why would you not drink after me?"

" But, mademoiselle, I had the honor of telling you: because I do not like milk."

" Don't fib—it was another lesson! When we get up to ten, we will make a cross, won't we? However, I don't bear you any grudge. No, seriously, I feel that I gain a great deal in your company, commandant. A little more of this discipline, and I shall be a perfection."

There was more truth than she thought, doubtless, in that pleasantry. She has a great respect for M. d'Éblis, and is very much on her guard before him. She watches carefully, in spite of herself, to see how he will look upon her pranks, and often checks herself in the midst of a frolic, if she notices the slightest sign of disapproval on his face. She chafes a little at the curb, but she recognizes her master and obeys him. In short, she submits in a very great degree, as every one does for that matter, to the authority of this firm and tender character, this lofty and somewhat disdainful spirit. The companionship of M. d'Éblis, if she could enjoy it constantly, would be very salutary to her. Only he and I have such a command over her. Ah! if ever—if ever the dream with which I flatter myself should be realized—the dear creature always surrounded by the friendship and the influence of us both, would truly become, as she says, "a perfection"—and a most pleasing perfection.

July 26th.

I am still much moved and agitated by a conversation that I have just had with Cécile. Feeling the reproaches that she addressed to me the other day, I had heartily resumed the course of my observations and studies of the merits of MM. de Valnesse. After due reflection, my choice was fixed upon M. René, who seemed to me to have a less superficial nature and a more cultivated mind than his cousin Henri. Immediately after breakfast I said significantly to Cécile that I would like to speak with her. "Very well!" said she, dryly, "what about?" "Really! why, of what interests you so much." "Nothing 'interests me so much!' However, let us hear."

A little surprised by this beginning, I led her under the fir-trees of the park. "Well, my dear," I said to her, "my choice is made."

"Ah! You have taken a great deal of time for it!"

"The choice will be all the wiser," I returned, laughingly. Then I recounted to her my long hesitation, and finally enumerated all the reasons which seemed to me to incline the balance in favor of M. René.

She listened to me with a strange air, her lips pressed together, her eyes roving about, and striking here and there the trunks of the trees with the end of her parasol. When I had finished—

"Unfortunately, I prefer the other."

"What other?"

"Whom but M. Henri, naturally?"

"The misfortune is not very great, my darling,

4

for, as I have told you, I see hardly any differences between these two gentlemen that are tangible, only shadows; and, in this equality of suitability and merit, it is very clear that it is your own personal taste that should decide."

"For yourself," resumed Cécile, "you would marry M. René?"

"He is not addressing himself to me!"

"But, in short, you would marry him if you were free to?"

"No."

"Why?"

"Because I don't love him."

"That is to say, he would not be worthy of you; but he is good enough for me!"

"My dear," replied I, tranquilly, "if you choose, we will resume our conversation at some time when you are in a better humor."

"No," said she, twirling her parasol, "it is only that I find it a truly incredible thing—it wounds me—this furor among you all to be rid of me; my father, my aunt, and even you! However, I am not your slave. Girls cannot be married by force; and I say to you distinctly, my dear, as I have said to my father and my aunt—I do not wish to marry."

"As for that," said I, "nothing is easier, my dear child."

"I would prefer a thousand times to reënter the convent."

"Pardon me, my dear, it is not a convent that you should enter, but a private hospital. Meanwhile, I will reënter my room."

I walked away, for my patience, which is very great, was at an end. She held me back by my arm. "Charlotte, do not leave me; I am unhappy!" and, in her affectionate way, she threw herself weeping into my arms.

I was profoundly troubled, for her words, "I am unhappy!" had roused a startling suspicion in my mind. But at last I murmured through the caresses that I lavished on her: "What has happened? What is the matter?"

She answered me, shaking her head and stammering out the words brokenly, "Nothing—nothing—I do not know—truly I do not know."

When I saw that she had recovered herself a little, I pressed her anew with questions; she looked

at me fixedly a moment, as if she were on the point
of confiding some secret to me; then she sighed
and was silent.

At last she was able to give me some such explanation of her emotion as this: As long as she saw
her marriage in the distant horizon, she said to me,
she regarded it with the indifference of a child; but,
in proportion as it appeared in a nearer and more
real perspective, she understood its serious character
better, and she recoiled from the choice which must
carry with it the happiness or unhappiness of her
whole life. She concluded by begging me to leave
her a few days more for reflection.

I simply observed to her that she had submitted
these gentlemen to a rather long novitiate, and that,
if she remained much longer without manifesting a
preference for one or the other, she might see them
both depart some fine morning discouraged.

"Ah, well, good riddance to them!" said Cécile.

We returned to the house, and I went immediately to my room; I was in haste to be alone, to try to
put my ideas into calm order. I have not succeeded;
my head and my heart are bewildered. It is not possible for me to mistake Cécile's feelings; there are

not two ways of interpreting her quite new indifference to the regard of the MM. de Valnesse, her
words, her silence, her tears. She loves, or she believes she loves, M. d'Éblis. That is her secret! Great
God, is it possible? Of all the griefs that I could
suffer, of all the afflictions that my imagination could
conceive, assuredly this would be one of the most
bitter. A rivalry of the heart, a contest of jealousy
between Cécile and me! A contest in which I
must sacrifice either my dearest friendship or my
dearest love! What a trial!—and I cannot even
pray to God to spare me: it has come; it exists.

I have done my best; I have tried my utmost to
elevate my thoughts. I cannot willingly share his
love—I cannot! All that I can do—and I will do
it—is to bring to this sad contest an integrity, an
irreproachable loyalty, not to say a word prejudicial
to Cécile, not one word that shall advance my interests; to wait finally, with a torn heart but peaceful
conscience, till he chooses between us two. If he
should choose me at last, Cécile would without
doubt suffer cruelly, poor girl! However, I believe
—I know so well her lively, tender, but fickle nature—she would find consolation, and I—never!

From the beginning, his inclination carried him
toward me rather than toward her. A woman does
not deceive herself in these things. Besides, my
grandmother remarked it; and, finally, although I
am far from boasting of it, there is, it seems to me,
between us, between our characters, more sympathy
and harmony. Since that happy evening when we
came to understand each other so well, I have found
him, it is true, colder, and more reserved with me;
but there has been something on his mind. He appears also a little more engrossed with, or rather
more curious about, Cécile; but she amuses him, I
believe, more than she pleases him. However, who
knows? Ah! my poor darling, what an injury you
have done me!

They are calling me for the afternoon excursion.
M. d'Éblis will accompany us. Now that my eyes
are opened, the least circumstance, the smallest detail, will be a decisive revelation.

Same day, Evening.

In the course of this excursion, Cécile met with
a singular adventure. We took the carriages about
two o'clock to pay a visit to the curé of Louvercy,

who had arranged a fishing-party for us. His parsonage, which adjoins the church, is only a few kilo-
metres from the château, and is situated on the bank
of a little river that is, I think, a tributary of the
Eure. Half of the party repaired to the parsonage
garden, which juts out into the river so as to seem
almost like an island, and betook themselves to fishing. M. d'Éblis, Mme. de Chagres, her husband,
and myself, remained in the churchyard, which is
one of the prettiest village churchyards anywhere to
be seen. The church itself, lost in the trees, is a
graceful fifteenth-century monument whose porch
and pointed-arched windows are covered with pretty
fretwork. M. d'Éblis set himself to draw it. We
had brought seats and formed a group about him,
watching his work, and admiring by turns the play
of the light on the water and amid the foliage, for
the day was glorious. At the end of the road which
skirts the churchyard, there is an old wooden bridge
thrown across the river, and opposite on the other
side of the water a rocky hill crowned with green
grass. We surveyed it all seated in the shade of a
venerable yew which, under the heat of the day,
emitted a resinous odor.

Soon we saw Cécile appear; she had quickly got tired of fishing—and perhaps also of M. d'Éblis's absence. She came to flutter and hover around him like a butterfly; then she began to stroll through the churchyard and read the epitaphs in an undertone. But there was one thing that especially attracted her attention, and before long absorbed her completely. Some one in the village had died; and in the middle of the churchyard a grave had been dug, doubtless to be filled to-morrow morning. This open grave awakened Cécile's interest in an extraordinary degree. After approaching it several times with mingled dread and curiosity, she grew bolder little by little, and tried to look into the bottom of it. But that was difficult, for on all sides of the grave masses of earth and gravel which had been dug out of it were piled up and gave way underfoot. Finally, an idea occurred to her: to enable her to lean over the grave without risk, she seized firmly the top of a little cypress, which grew on a hillock near by, with one hand, and leaning with the other on her parasol, we saw her bend her fragile form over the grave and look eagerly into its depths. M. d'Éblis raised his head; he took in at a glance this strange scene, lighted up by the summer's sun, this charming figure leaning over this sinister hole, this young and fresh face, half smiling, half terrified. He turned the leaf of his portfolio over hastily, to fix this memory on the next page at once. Then, suddenly springing to his feet, he cried: "Take care, mademoiselle! for Heaven's sake, take care!"

We all rose with the same impulse. The cypress by which Cécile supported herself with one hand had been half undermined that morning by the grave-digger's work, and it yielded with her weight at the same instant that the rubbish gave way under her feet. She lost her balance, threw up her arms, uttered a scream, and disappeared in the yawning grave!

We hurried to her with feelings which it is difficult for me to describe. I felt, myself, as if a stroke of lightning had shot through me from head to foot. We reached her very quickly. The poor girl had got up, and was standing at the bottom of the grave, her hair disordered, immovable, utterly bewildered, and looking up at us with a ludicrous smile. The Valnesses had rushed up, like ourselves, at the scream she had uttered. Amid great confusion, everybody proffered his advice for getting her out of this terrible tomb. They stretched out their hands to her, but in vain. Every one knows how deep these graves are. Some of the gentlemen said it would be necessary to go for ropes, others suggested chairs and a ladder; meanwhile Cécile appeared to be in a state of hysterical exaltation, which would easily become dangerous if prolonged.

The calm and commanding voice of M. d'Éblis silenced every one. He waved us back with a gesture. " Come, mademoiselle," he said, laughing, " let us not lose our heads. There is nothing serious in this accident. A little coolness and you will be out of that in a minute. Gymnastics are my strong point, as you shall see. Now listen! Let me pass my hands under your arms." He half knelt on the *débris* and lifted Cécile by the shoulders, smiling at her and encouraging her with a look; and then, raising himself gradually, he set her down on the ground. But at that moment she fainted; her eyes closed, and she lay motionless in his arms, pale as a corpse, her lips half open.

" She mustn't find herself here when she comes to herself," said M. d'Éblis to us. " I am going to carry her to that apple-orchard down there; it is more cheerful."

Accordingly, he went out of the churchyard, bearing the swooning Cécile on his breast. We let down the bars of the apple-orchard on the other side of the road for him. As he bent over to lay her gently on the grass, she opened her eyes and looked at him for a second or two in a dazed way; then recollecting herself and smiling at him, she murmured, "A father to me." Then, instantly closing her eyes, she fainted anew. Water was brought; I bathed her temples and loosened her corsage slightly, and she soon came to her senses. A quarter of an hour afterward we set out to return to the château. On the way we tried with affectionate pleasantry to make light of the adventure, and laughed over it heartily, but without succeeding in totally dissipating the superstitious impression that it had left upon Cécile's mind. Although she did her best to laugh with us, she remained very pale and pensive.

Nevertheless, it is possible that she will owe her happiness to this doleful incident. I was walking at M. d'Éblis's side when he was carrying her in his arms, and I could see the expression of his face bent over this pretty, sleeping head. It was not altogether sympathy and compassion; it was the tenderest admiration. Undoubtedly, in the very weakness of this delicate being, always in need of protection, there is a powerful attraction for a strong soul.

Ah! Cécile, Providence is on thy side!

July 30th.

Nothing very new. Cécile has submitted more and more to the power and the charm of M. d'Éblis; that is evident, and every one is beginning to notice it. As for him, I do not know what to think. He is an enigma. In his manner with Cécile, there is certainly an aroused and amused curiosity, pleasure, a lively interest, affection even, but no passion, as it seems to me: nothing as ardent—if I dare say so—as one of those looks which I found fixed on me so often formerly, and which I still hope to suddenly surprise some time. Even his voice in speaking to me is strangely troubled, as it never is with Cécile. What can be passing in this heart?

I went to walk in the park this morning, ques-

tioning myself the while; and, in questioning myself, I confess I cried a little, and I do not weep
very easily, either. But this constant and sustained
agitation to which I am a prey, this secret rivalry
with my best friend, these internal struggles between
my conscience and my duty, between my unhappy
passion and my disturbed friendship, all this martyrdom—for that is just what it is—has shaken my
nerves frightfully. At the turning of the lonely
path where I was walking I suddenly saw Mme. de
Louvercy appear. She had her handkerchief in her
hand, and seemed to me to be using it as I had
mine. She, too, had just been weeping. She could
not recover herself as quickly as I. "You surprise
me," she said, "in one of my moments of deep discouragement."

"Is M. Roger suffering again, madame?" I
asked.

"Not physically, but his moral condition makes
me despair. I have believed for several days, ever
since he consented to seek a little distraction in our
society, that there was something to be hoped for
there; but it was an illusion. I imagine that this
very return to the world has, on the contrary, caused

him to feel still more keenly the severity of his misfortunes, exasperated his grief and his humiliation. You cannot know—but I am a daily witness of it all—the paroxysms of rebellious rage, the furiousness of a fallen angel, which shock me as a mother and, alas! as a Christian. Ah, my dear child," added she, taking me by the hands, "in such adversity we have only God! And he does not believe it, or, what is perhaps worse, he will not. He shuns a church like a leper. If he could only pray once, I feel that he would be comforted, if not consoled. But he will not; and yet he loves me much, though since his misfortune I have never been able to get him to pray. I have begged him on my knees, and he will not." And the poor woman burst into a flood of weeping. We stood there, looking sadly at each other, finding some sort of solace in drawing together both our sad hearts.

August 1st.

This day will count in my life. As there has been less animation at the château for some time past, no excursion was arranged for to-day, and every one remained at home, each in his own room or

in the *salon.* After scribbling the foregoing lines,
I thought of returning to that melancholy walk
where I had met Mme. de Louvercy, and resuming
the reverie she had interrupted. I was on my way
thither when I heard a sound of rapid footsteps
behind me; I turned around and saw M. d'Éblis.
"Pardon me, mademoiselle," he said, with his
gravest air, "will you honor me with a few moments' conversation?"

At these words, my heart stopped short; and,
when it began to beat again, the shock was so violent that my very being seemed on the point of dis-
solution. I realized that the moment had come,
and that the sentence of my fate was to be pronounced.

"Monsieur," I replied, dissembling my emotion
as best I could, though very badly, I fear, "I am
listening."

He was very much agitated himself; he walked
a few steps at my side in silence. Then he resumed : "Mademoiselle, I shall seem very indiscreet
to you, but my indiscretion will at least prove the
profound and respectful confidence with which you
have inspired me, since I shall trust to you for the

happiness or the misery of my existence. More than any one else in the world, mademoiselle, you are in a position to know Mlle. Cécile de Stèle thoroughly. You were friends in childhood. You were companions at the convent, were you not?"

" Yes, monsieur."

" You have had an opportunity of intimately studying and estimating her character, her mind. Before offering her my hand, before consecrating my life to her, may I ask you what you think of her?"

" Everything good."

" You feel, do you not, mademoiselle, that there is nothing conventional in my questions? I conjure you, let your reply be equally sincere. Mlle. de Stèle is a very attractive young girl—any one can see that—graceful and full of distinction; brilliant and *spirituelle*—I know all that. But her character is a little anomalous and inconsistent: it surprises me; it even startles me a little, I confess. In a word, I ask you, who have been able to penetrate all its mysteries, what is there to hope for in it, and what to dread?"

" Cécile, monsieur, has never known a mother.

She has been brought up by her father, whose only child she is, and who has spoiled her at once a little and a great deal. This is the explanation of the inequalities of temperament, the contradictions, the caprices that have struck you. But her nature is admirable. She is the tenderest, the most constant, the most devoted of friends; she will be the most tender, constant, and devoted of wives—on one condition, that she is well guided and loves her guide."

"I ask a thousand pardons," he rejoined, "but do you believe that she can love a man whose character is as different from her own as mine is, for example; a man whose serious and almost severe bearing contrasts so strongly with her sprightliness —at least apparently? You do not reply."

"Because I am seeking my words, not my thought; for my opinion does not waver. I believe, then, monsieur, that if there is any one especially fitted to win Cécile, to reform her little failings, to develop still further her noble qualities, to make her an honorable, faithful, and happy woman, it is yourself."

He bowed low. Then after a pause, "More

than all, you are very fond of her, are you not ?" he
asked.

"Very."

"That itself is a high encomium.   Thank you,
mademoiselle ; I receive her with absolute confidence
from your hand."

We had been drawing near the château ; he took
the path thither after having again thanked me, and
saluted me with a gesture and a glance.   When he
had disappeared from my sight, I sat down on one
of the benches of the path.   After having supported myself throughout this interview by an effort of
courage and pride, I felt the ground sinking beneath
me.

It was all over: from that instant, my life was
desolate ; my heart, though only twenty years old,
had received a wound that will never heal.

But how understand such conduct in a man of
honor—a man of taste, moreover ?   By what secret
inspiration, by what refinement of cruelty, could he
have been actuated ?   I cannot conceive.

Had he any consciousness of the horrible torture
he was inflicting upon me ?   I know not.   All I
know is, this is how it happened.

At his first words, at the first blow, I fixed my mind on only one thing—to save my womanly dignity in his eyes, and to conquer the impulse of base jealousy which urged me to slander Cécile. Perhaps this preoccupation was excessive, and so I was drawn into a eulogy contrary to my belief and to the truth. But error in this direction is better than error in the other. Meanwhile I had not got to the end of the trials the day had in store for me.

When I was able to stand on my feet, I began to walk again, to try and calm my agitation. I walked on straight before me without knowing whither, and, as I was crossing one of the principal avenues of the park, a noise of wheels caused me to look around. It was M. Roger de Louvercy, in his *panier*. He was alone, for, in spite of his mother's urgent request, he generally refuses to take a servant with him, following his habit of declining all assistance save when it is an absolute necessity.

He was driving rapidly, after his usual fashion. Seeing me, he reined in his spirited horse with difficulty, checking it almost in the air within two paces of me. "Will you not take a drive, mademoiselle?"

he asked, with his always ironical and slightly bitter smile.

" No, thank you."

" Is it my horse or myself that frightens you ? "

" Neither."

" Well, in that case give me the pleasure of your company."

" It seems to me," I said, " that it would hardly be very proper."

" Oh, proper ! " replied he, shaking his head. " Alas ! with me nothing is improper. Besides, we will not go out of our own woods. Come !—you will not ? Undoubtedly I horrify you ! "

I saw the habitual pallor and melancholy of his face deepen. I was seized with a lively sentiment of pity ; and then at the time any kind of diversion was a welcome relief. My head was half crazed, and everything was the same to me.

" If it is only for a drive in the park," I said, " I shall be very glad to go."

Then I got up into the *panier*, not without making the attempt twice, for the horse, a jet-black thorough-bred, was very restive, and M. de Louvercy had great difficulty in holding it with his one hand. Then we set off at a very rapid pace. Very soon, "You have missed your vocation, mademoiselle," said M. de Louvercy, smiling.

"How?"

"You were born to be a Sister of Charity. There was one in the Orleans Hospital, while I was there, who resembles you a little. That struck me the first time I saw you. But she was less beautiful. Are you of creole origin?"

"No, I am a Parisian. This Sister took good care of you?"

"Too good," he replied, with a sigh.

"Why too good?"

"What good was it to preserve a life which must be only a burden to myself and every one else?"

"Will you let me tell you, monsieur, that you seem to me a little unjust toward Providence? Providence has cruelly afflicted you, beyond doubt, but are you not too insensible to the consolations which it has left you, and which so many unfortunates are without?"

"Pray, what consolations, mademoiselle?"

"Your mother, first of all, and her incomparable

tenderness; then the solicitude of so rare and devoted a friendship; finally, study—the leisure you
have to read, the delight that it gives you, the rec-
ognition and esteem that it promises—"

" Yes," he rejoined, bitterly; " all that may prevent me from going mad. But that is all it can do.
And still there are moments when I think I am
mad, or when I am in reality."

He was silent for a few seconds, shaking the
reins abstractedly and worrying the mouth of his
horse, which certainly did not need to be excited.
He did not perceive at first that the animal fretted,
and was getting the better of his hand, and he resumed : " You saw D'Éblis this morning ? "

" Yes; he had just left me when you ran across
me."

" Ah ! A noble fellow, is he not ? "

" Yes," I replied, with a simple nod. He looked
steadily at me.

" You are very pale, mademoiselle. I had already noticed it. Are you suffering ? "

" No."

There was a wicked smile on his lips, and, as if
he had done it purposely, he again shook the reins

on the back of his horse, which became half fren-
zied. We fairly flew. The horse, in his furious and
reckless course, just escaped dashing us against the
bars of the avenue gateway, turned violently to the
right, and tore along at a frightful rate on a public
road leading, although I did not know it, to a wash-
house on the river-border, which is very steep in
this place.

M. de Louvercy endeavored to quiet his horse
with hand and voice, but he did not succeed; we
sped on like the wind; the trees waltzed by like vi-
sions: a kind of vertigo seized me. We drew near
the end of the road, and already saw the sun's reflection in the water.

M. de Louvercy turned to me. "'Mlle. Charlotte," he said, coldly, with that insane look that he
has in his bad moments, "do you value life greatly?"

Truly not. I did not value it highly. A simple movement of my eyebrows told him as much.

"All the same," he replied; "it would be a
pity!"

I don't know if he had a secret wherewith to
tame his horse, which he had not chosen to employ
before; but almost immediately, obedient to a word

or two, accompanied by a slight movement of the
hand, the animal became quiet; he resumed a reasonable gait, and we were able before reaching the
river to turn aside into the fork of another road.

M. de Louvercy, whose coolness I had admired
in spite of everything—for we had certainly run
the risk of our necks—then said to me, quietly: "It
is easy enough to understand why I do not care for
life; but you! It is a mystery!"

"It is a mystery," I repeated, smiling.

"A disappointment in love?" he retorted, in a
tone of sombre irony; and after a pause, "So lovely—yet disdained—that would be strange!"

"Monsieur," I said, very sharply, "your misfortune gives you great privileges, but it does not,
I presume, allow you the liberty of insulting a
woman."

"Have I not told you that I was insane?"

"I see it, monsieur; but I should have been
warned of it."

He was silent for a long time. He bit his lips,
so that I saw a drop of blood spurt from them.
Finally, he resumed in a greatly moved voice:
"Mademoiselle, I am unworthy of the honor you

have done me. I feel it, and I humbly beg you to forgive me."

"Very well, monsieur. Shall we return?"

We were then far out in the country; I could see the little church of Louvercy through the trees.

"We will return," he said, sadly; "but for Heaven's sake, shall we return angry with each other—enemies? Mademoiselle, is there anything in the world that a poor wretch like myself can do for you to show his profound respect and to efface the memory of a hateful word?"

A sudden idea occurred to me. I remembered what Mme. de Louvercy had told me in the morning of the grief which the rebellious impiety of her son caused her. I saw the little church close by us, and said, hastily: "Yes, you can do something which will win back my esteem and deserve my friendship. There is the church down there; come and pray with me there."

His brows suddenly contracted; nevertheless he asked in a gentle voice:

"Has my mother been speaking to you?"

"Yes."

"Do you wish it?"

5

" Yes."

" Let us go."

A few minutes after, we reached the garden
of the parsonage which adjoins the church. The
curé's servant at work in the garden raised his head
at the noise; M. de Louvercy called to him and
asked him to hold his horse. I got down and helped
him to alight. Then we entered the churchyard,
and passed under the pointed-arched porch, to the
lively surprise of the servant, who was not accustomed to see M. Roger within these precincts.

The interior of the church is very simple ; a
small nave, white and bare. I walked before M.
de Louvercy, whose crutch resounded on the pave-
ment and under the vaulted arches. We proceeded
through two rows of seats to the place reserved for
Mme. de Louvercy. I pointed to a low bench covered with a cushion, and said to him in a whisper,
" Your mother's *prie-dieu.*" Then I supported
him by the arm while he knelt on it ; he abandoned
himself like an infant. He leaned his head on his
hand, and I knelt at his side. While I prayed for
us both with all my soul, his heart softened and I
heard him sobbing.

When we arose he said to me, letting me see his streaming face, "See what you have made a soldier do!"

"And you are pardoned," I replied, taking his hand.

Soon after we departed, rapidly as always, but not with reckless speed. His emotion calmed; he became almost gay, and questioned the peasants whom we met here and there on the way, informing himself in their affairs, and relating their history to me with interest. I had known before, however, that his misanthropy did not prevent him from doing much good in the country, where he is really liked.

We had just entered the park, when we saw at the turning of a path three persons walking slowly before us: they were Mme. de Louvercy, M. d'Éblis, and Cécile. They appeared greatly surprised to see me with M. Roger.

"Mother," he cried, laughing, "I meant to elope with Mlle. d'Erra, and it is she who has run away with me. And do you know where she took me? No, you do not suspect. Come, I want to leave her the pleasure of telling you herself."

I jumped to the ground, and taking Mme. de Louvercy, who seemed more and more mystified, aside, I whispered to her: "I took him to church; he has prayed."

She uttered a cry; and, clasping me to her heart with a kind of violence, she exclaimed, "Ah, my dear, dear child!" And then, after a pause and a long sigh: "Now I have all my happiness at once, for—do you know? Cécile—" and she pointed to her, standing near M. d'Éblis.

"Yes, I know," I said.

"Who would ever have thought that she would make such a wise choice; and that he, on his side— well, surely God has his own days!"

Cécile, meanwhile, had taken my arm; and she said to her aunt, in a pleading tone, "Leave me alone with her."

Mme. de Louvercy and M. d'Éblis then left us, conversing tenderly with M. Roger, who was walking his horse. Cécile drew me along, and, following a short, winding path, made me enter with her a very retired part of the park which they call the Hermitage. The tradition of the country has it that there was formerly in this place the abode of a hermit, evidences of whose presence are supposed to have been found in some *débris* of masonry, to-day half covered by a hillock of greensward. The lonely ruin, almost intact, is a very small and very old building in the form of a round arch, under whose shelter gushes into a narrow reservoir the source of a brook which runs through the wood. There is a bit of ground large enough to have been the garden of the ruined habitation, which now forms a smooth lawn, a kind of promenade in which are here and there groups of lofty trees. The place is of a singularly sweet and yet savage aspect, a sort of sacred vale of grateful solitude, in which one thinks of the nooks in those landscapes wherein are depicted the sports of nymphs and shepherds around some antique fountain.

Cécile led me thither in silence; then, looking at me with uneasy tenderness and bathed in tears, clasping me round the neck, she cried, " Ah! I have stolen him from you—I have stolen him from you!"

I mingled my tears with hers, returning her caresses and murmuring: "What folly! What are you thinking of? Do not spoil your happiness by such a fancy."

"You have been so good to me," she pursued, weeping, "so generous! He told me. Ah! you, only, are worthy of him—you, only! You did not love him *too* much—tell me?"

"No, indeed, dear; be calm: it was sympathy solely."

"But I—I adore him! Listen: it was here, in this lovely retreat, that he told me he loved me, that he asked me if I would be his wife. I should like to be buried here when I die; do you believe it would be possible?"

"I do not know, pet; but you say very absurd things do you know?"

"Indeed, I think I am a little crazy. But will he be happy with me; do you believe he will? I want him to be happy—oh! so much."

"He will be happy, dear."

In a word, nothing has been spared me. I cut this recital short, for my heart fails me.

Meanwhile, what am I going to do? I shall see to-morrow. I shall consult my grandmother. I have determined to tell her everything.

August 2d.

My grandmother learned last evening, as all the château did, the grand news of Cécile's engagement. Although certainly surprised and even in the highest degree indignant, she received the announcement with a calm serenity and a smile that set me a good example. To me she simply said, in leaving me on the staircase, "This gentleman has singular taste!"

This morning she anticipated me, and entered my room just as I awoke from a short sleep. After kissing me and clasping my hand tightly, she said : "My dear little girl, Mmes. de Sauves and de Chagres have just told me that they leave to-day with their brothers. Their conduct seems to me utterly ridiculous; it is a confession of their disappointment and spite ; it is pitifully despicable. We have more pride than that, have we not, little one ?"

"Yes, grandmamma."

"We know how to suffer with dignity ; and, though it will be irksome, we will stay here a fortnight or three weeks longer to preserve our self-respect. At least, that is my advice. Do you feel brave enough ?"

"I will try."

"Besides, little one, flight in such a case is no more reasonable than it is dignified. It is best to look things in the face, and get used to them. Don't you think so?"

"I don't know, any more."

"Well, you will see. If it proves beyond your strength, we will go. Forgive me, child, if I am a little brutal with your grief, instead of petting you; really it is wiser. Trouble ought never to be cherished. Kiss me; I love you very dearly, child;" and she went to her own room to relent by herself, I think.

As for my meditations during the night, this is the result of them: I have so often, in society, heard eternal love ridiculed and constancy called a fable—above all, that of my own sex—that I find it a little difficult to believe myself an exception in this respect; still it is impossible for me to conceive that my heart, even in the most distant future, will ever open itself to a sentiment which shall expel that which I have already admitted there; right or wrong, I am sure that I shall always love the man whom I have once loved with all my heart, all my mind, all the power of my being and my life. It is not even possible, with such a sentiment in my heart, to imagine myself united to another. Unless I become greatly changed, which I neither expect nor desire, I shall never marry. As long as my grandmother is left to me, I shall live with her and for her. If I outlive her, I shall return to the convent in which I passed my youth, never to leave it. I feel that there I shall not be hopelessly unhappy ; I shall take there bitter regrets, no doubt, but I shall find consolation there. Apart even from the poetry of the cloister and the sweet nearness of divine things, I shall find in my humble duties of instructress the illusion of maternal devotion, although I must always realize that it is an illusion. What I have done hitherto for Cécile, I shall do for others, and they will be my family.

With this plan for the future, I shall for the present obey the wishes of my grandmother ; my own pride sympathizes with hers. I should blush to betray a mortifying disappointment by a hasty departure. Doubtless I shall suffer much ; but of this kind of suffering I experienced yesterday all that one can have, I think.

My grandmother has had a long interview with Mme. de Louvercy to-day. What it was about I cannot divine, but the result of it apparently has been a modification of our plans. Instead of leaving a fortnight hence, we go to-morrow. She has just told me, saying that we have done all that our dignity demands. Her features showed great anxiety, and Mme. de Louvercy, when I saw her leave my grandmother's room, was very much discomposed. Nothing, however, happened between them that wounded either of them; their attitude toward each other proves that; it is affectionate and even tender, although stamped with a peculiar melancholy. I give up the attempt to penetrate this fresh mystery; indeed, it disturbs me very little; its importance to me is that we owe our departure to it. I had, I confess, presumed too much on my courage; it is exhausted. The departure of the Valnesses and their sisters left me frequently alone with the two lovers; I was the smiling witness of their *tête-à-têtes*, their endearments, their happiness—the smiling and despairing witness. Jealousy is a frightfully complicated pang; it not only tears the heart, it degrades it. One feels not only tortured but abased. The wound is not open, it is not wholesome ; the ulcers of pride, envy, hatred, mingle in it, rankle in it, defile it. \ There is no passionate soul, I suppose, that is not, in such a cursed hour, capable of such unworthy feelings ; the merit consists not in being incapable of them, but in abhorring and conquering them./ With God's aid I have tried to do that—but I am glad we are going.

I promised Cécile to return for her marriage, if she is married here, but I imagine that the ceremony will take place in Paris, and I much prefer that it should.

M. de Louvercy did not breakfast with us this morning. He will not come to dinner this evening. He is suffering seriously, it appears. I have remarked that for some days his manner was more languid and ailing than usual. I am sorry to go away without seeing him again. I shall never see him again probably, for he does not leave Louvercy, and I hope never to return to it. Poor fellow! I shall always appreciate what he did for me.

August 9th.

What a night !

Looking after our packing kept me on my feet till one o'clock in the morning. I had just sent away my maid, and was beginning to undress, when I thought I heard a door, on the landing opposite mine, cautiously opened, then a light footstep, a creaking of the wainscoting, the rustle of silk on the steps; some one was descending the staircase very softly. Surprised and filled with a strange terror that I could not analyze, I opened my door gently, and saw a faint light at the bottom of the staircase; at the same time a murmur of words uttered in broken accents, and what seemed to me stifled groans, ascended to where I stood. I leaned over the rail, and could just recognize Mme. de Louvercy, who had paused, a candle in her hand, on the ground-floor landing; she was leaning her forehead against the door of her son's room, and listening intently. Suddenly she opened the door warily and glided into the apartment.

I stood there, restless and palpitating, for two or three minutes, when a woman's cry—a sharp, grief-stricken cry—broke the deep silence of the night.

I started forward, descending the staircase recklessly, and reached the door which Mme. de Louvercy had left ajar. It opens into a sort of study, which leads into M. Roger's room. The study was plunged in darkness, but a ray of light penetrated thither across the passage which separated it from the adjoining room. I listened anxiously in my turn, and my heart beat violently. Mme. de Louvercy had entered the room ; she was sobbing, and her voice broke out at intervals in accents of despairing entreaty. No voice replied. I was seized with a mortal terror ; I believed some terrible misfortune had happened. Almost without reflection, I entered the study and raised noiselessly a corner of the *portière.* Before me was M. Roger de Louvercy, seated in an arm-chair near a table ; he had the rigidity and the pallor of a ghost, and looked with a fixed and speechless stare at his unhappy mother, who lay prostrate before him, her hands clasped, and striking her forehead against the knees of her son. I could see on the table a large letter sealed with wax, and near it one of those oblong boxes of violet ebony which contain costly pistols. Finally, M. Roger muttered, in a dull and irritated tone, "Jean would have done better to have held his tongue!" (Jean is an old soldier, who is now his confidential servant.)

"Oh, I pray you, I pray you!" replied Mme. de Louvercy, midst her sobs. "Am I nothing to you—nothing to you? O my God!"

He still hesitated. Then I saw him bend down and take his mother's head in his hand and kiss her forehead. "Pardon," he said; "this hour of madness is over—wholly passed, I promise you."

"You promise me—you promise me truly, my dear child?"

"I promise you—only let her go, I beg of you; let me not see her again!"

"Yes, yes, that is right; you know she goes to-morrow—this very morning."

"And she shall never know of this?"

"Never! Oh, no!"

"Then good-night, mother; rest in peace. Once more forgive me; go in peace. You have my word; I swear it to you—I swear it! Take these away with you, if you wish."

While they clasped each other in a tight embrace, I went out hastily; I mounted the staircase and returned to my room. The remainder of the night I spent in strange reflections.

When day dawned, I went to my grandmother's room, and had a long conversation with her. She tried to tell me at first why Mme. de Louvercy wished to hasten our departure. It was useless; I knew it already.

I am going to sleep a little, and then I will resume.

Same day.

The resolution I had taken last night was long and strenuously opposed by my grandmother. "Dear child," she said to me, "you know that in theory I am not hostile to romance; but this is really too much! At your age, with your face, your figure, your education, your fortune, to marry an invalid is certainly very noble, very generous, very poetic; but, frankly, it transcends all bounds! And even if you had taken such a resolution at an ordinary time, in complete freedom of mind and heart, calmly and coolly, in full possession of yourself— well, it would be better. But this is not the case. You have just suffered a disenchantment—a very keen deception. Good Heavens! I shall never un-

derstand what that gentleman could have been thinking of, by-the-way.   Be that as it may, you are, dear
girl, in one of those states which engender false vo-
cations.   You must not trust too much to a first impulse of enthusiasm, which perhaps is only an impulse of despair.   At least let us wait—let us wait
a few months; let us allow time to pass upon this
notion.   If it is confirmed, if it grows stronger, then
—well, we shall see!   But, truly, I should not be
doing my duty if I allowed you to engage in such
a venture under the influence of your wounded
heart, and of the emotion which last night's tragic
scene has excited in you."

Briefly summed up, these are the objections of
my grandmother.   I opposed them in my turn with
all my conviction and all my eloquence : Undoubtedly, I was a little romantic ; but had she not herself
encouraged this tendency in me ?   Had she not told
me it was a guarantee of self-respect, and even of
happiness ?   Undoubtedly, my heart was bruised and
sick ; but had not a stricken heart need of a great
duty and a generous devotion to relieve and sustain
it ?   Ought it not to find consolation and oblivion of
its own lost happiness solely in the happiness of

others? I did not conceal from her my design of some day entering the convent, if I should ever be unfortunate enough to find myself alone in the world; and, thinking solely of sacrifice, was not that, the opportunity to make which was here presented to me, loftier, more pious, more touching, less selfish even, than the mere renunciation of the world and the somewhat commonplace abnegation of an instructress? As for waiting, that would be to risk, perhaps, all the merit and benevolence of my act. Who knew if, in the interval, this unhappy young man would not relapse into one of those fits of despair to which I had just seen him a prey; who could tell if his mother would again be forewarned, if he would not succumb? One thing at least was certain, that to wait would deprive me of the best part of my reward—the joy, namely, that I promised myself in witnessing the sudden transport of these poor people from the excess of misery to an unhoped-for happiness, in being the cause of it, in descending suddenly into their sombre life as an angel of light: that single moment of my existence would throw over the past, the present, and the future, a peace, a charm, and an infinite consolation.

My dear grandmother, with fast-flowing tears, readily replied to my arguments. "Alas! poor little girl," she murmured in conclusion, "the world will say we are two fools."

"This is folly that God will bless," I rejoined.

"I believe it," said my grandmother, "but there is another difficulty that stares me in the face."

"What can that be, for Heaven's sake?"

"How are we to broach this matter to the Louvercys? I must do justice to the poor mother. When she confided to me the unhappy passion of her son, she did not seem for an instant to entertain the idea—truly an inconceivable one, by-the-way—of a marriage between you two. And the young man has evidently no conception of it, either; which does honor to his good sense—but then, what? Must we offer ourselves, leap into their arms without even crying, 'Take care!' My daughter, it is impossible; it is utterly improper."

"But, grandmamma, since we are sure they will not refuse us—?"

"Ah! good! That is all there is lacking in the matter. Well, it is a very delicate piece of business —very delicate."

" Will you intrust it to me, grandmamma ? "

" Why not, forsooth ? As well take an ell as an inch. Since we are up to our necks in irregularities, another more or less doesn't matter. Still, I fancy you will nevertheless first address yourself to the mother ? "

" Assuredly," I answered.

That is why I have just asked a moment's conversation with Mme. de Louvercy, and in a few minutes I shall be with her.

Same day.

Mme. de Louvercy was with her son when my message was brought to her. She came up to my room instantly. Her countenance, which is one of the noblest that I know, was still very pale and disfigured by the terrible emotions of the night ; nevertheless she smiled at me, though with a distracted air like that of a person whose thoughts were a thousand miles from the surprise I had in store for her. " My dear child," she said to me, " you want to bid me good-by ; you are very kind ; I am very glad myself to take leave of you without any witnesses, for I can better say to you alone how much I shall miss you, how much I thank you for having been so obliging, so compassionate, toward all of us."

She took my hands as she spoke; she saw that I was extremely troubled, and felt that I was trembling. Her anxious features suddenly became alert, and her eyes sought mine with an expression of wonder and vague suspicion.

"Madame," I said, stammering a little, "I have to ask your forgiveness for something. I was very indiscreet last night—"

She looked at me with a deeper and more intense scrutiny.

"I heard you pass—then I heard you weeping. I feared that you were in need of assistance; I descended—"

"You know all?" she cried, in her turn trembling from head to foot.

"I know all, yes. I am profoundly touched by the sentiments with which I have inspired your son, deeply touched also by his misfortune; in a word, madame"—and I drew near her very gently—"are you willing to accept me as a daughter?"

Her whole body shook with a sudden paroxysm; her eyes, dilated, stupefied, and almost wild, remained fixed on mine; her half-open lips moved tremulously. She murmured in a low tone, " No, it is not possible."

" Will you take me for your daughter? " I asked again, smiling.

Ah! what a cry she uttered! what a mother's cry, a happy mother's!

I have no very clear recollection of what passed in the few moments that followed. I had half lost my senses, and she also. She clasped me to her breast, kissed me, half stifled me, called me the tenderest names, praying, weeping, mingling my name with that of God in her transports of gratitude. Ah! how happy was that moment!

When she recovered a little and recollected herself she asked, with anxiety, " And your grandmother ? "

" She consents."

" Let us go to her." She drew me to my grandmother's room. After the first transports, very lively on both sides, my grandmother observed that, before we indulged our ecstasies further, it would perhaps be wise to discover the wishes of M. Roger

himself. "Good Heavens!" cried Mme. de Louvercy, "my poor boy—all that I ask is that he may
not die of joy; but I do not wish to delay his happiness longer." And catching sight of herself in
the mirror, with her lovely white hair disheveled,
"How I look!" she said; "he will think me crazy." She smoothed her hair a little, and walked
toward the door with the brisk and firm step of a
young girl: indeed, the light in her eyes, the glad
flush of her countenance, seemed to have suddenly
restored ten years to her. Upon the point of going
out, she stopped, and turning around, "He will
never believe me," she said; "truly, he will not
believe me," and she glanced timidly at me. I confess I was dying to go with her.

My grandmother, carried away by the enthusiasm of the moment, pushed me forward by the
shoulders. "Oh, run along, my dear; since we are
fairly swimming in impropriety—run along," she
cried.

Mme. de Louvercy passed her arm through mine
and drew me on, almost running. "What a contrast to this horrible night!" she said, embracing me
again as we descended the staircase. She opened

the door of the ground-floor apartment, and begged
me in a whisper to wait a moment in the study;
then she raised the *portière* and entered M. Roger's
room.

Hardly was I alone in the study when I was
sharply struck by the strangeness, and, to tell the
truth, by the impropriety, at least in appearance, of
my situation. I tried my best to recall everything
that could justify my procedure, everything excep-
tional that there was in the circumstances that had
guided me, in the unhappy state of M. Roger, and
the reserve it imposed on him; I tried to assure
myself that in the course of things the usual rôles
had been reversed; still I was not the less there, at
his very door, awaiting his good pleasure like an
Oriental slave, and, not being of a very humble
temperament, I was, to say the least, very uncom-
fortable. This uneasy feeling became more painful
in proportion as my solitude was prolonged, and
time was left me for reflection on which I had not
at all reckoned. My imagination had depicted this
scene to me as an exact repetition, lively and rapid,
of that which had so much moved me just before
—astonishment, a cry, a start, a transport! But, in-

stead of that, minutes succeeded minutes; I heard through the tapestry of the curtain low whispering, exchanges of confidences, a dialogue of discussion, a kind of formal debate. The blood left my heart and the floor swam under me, when at length the curtain was pushed aside, showing me the countenance of Mme. de Louvercy, not precisely sad, but serious and a little uneasy.

"Will you come in, my child?" she said, sweetly.

I entered the room. M. de Louvercy was standing, leaning his wounded knee on a chair; his features, whose usual expression is stormy and sarcastic, had utterly lost that character; a kind of grave and almost solemn melancholy proudly intensified their pure lines; his eyes, encircled with deep-blue furrows, seemed to me a little moist. He fixed his glance on me, and, speaking very slowly, as if to restrain an emotion that was almost bursting forth, he said:

"Mlle. Charlotte, my mother has informed me of the feeling of angelic kindness which brings you here. If I were less infirm than I am, I should be at your feet. I do not accept your sacrifice; but that the thought of it came to you is enough to comfort and charm my life, to make my gratitude most profound, most tender. It will follow you wherever you go, and bless you always. And now, mademoiselle, do not, I pray you, prolong a temptation that is truly beyond a man's strength to resist. Let me remain firm in the resolution which honor prescribes to me ; you will esteem me more highly —once more my thanks, and adieu ! "

He bowed very low. His mother was weeping silently.

I advanced a few steps toward him and put out my hand frankly. He took it and pressed it tightly. " My God ! " he said, in an undertone. Then, looking long at me, " Excuse me, mademoiselle ; I cannot find words ; my heart is so full, my mind so troubled ; I leap so suddenly from the very depths to heaven ! But at least let me prove to you how thoroughly sincere I was a moment ago, how much I feared to abuse an impulse of generosity, a transport of enthusiasm. You will take some time to reflect, I entreat you. In a few months—in a year, let us say—if you are of the same mind, if you are not more terrified at your great sacrifice than you are to-day—yes, I will accept it. But until that

6

time let me relieve you of all obligation, and return you your absolute freedom."

As he had kept my hand, I had no need of giving it to him to cement our agreement, with which Mme. de Louvercy appeared well satisfied, hoping, perhaps—and perhaps with reason—that it would have the same fate as many other modern treaties.

As for me, I replied simply: " As you choose, monsieur; but I shall not change. *Au revoir*—for the present—for you no longer stipulate that we depart to-day, I presume? You will grant us a reprieve of a few days?"

He nodded, smiling, and kissed my hand. Then his mother and I withdrew.

My grandmother, when she learned the result of this interview, declared that M. de Louvercy's conduct had been perfectly correct and honorable. I think the same; and, after having been so much shocked and mortified at the lack of eagerness with which he welcomed and replied to me, I feel that I should, nevertheless, have sincerely regretted it if he had acted otherwise. I appreciated him for his hesitation and his scruples, although I am sure, on reflection, that there is something further that he did not tell me. Yes, undoubtedly, he fears to abuse a sacrifice born of a romantic enthusiasm which is still subject to repentance; but he fears, also, to accept the gift of a wounded heart, which perhaps is not yet, and possibly never will be, healed of its wound. For it is certain that he at least suspects my attachment to M. d'Éblis. He could not ask an explanation of me; but, however delicate it may be, I shall explain it to him some day or other, and, as he is an honorable man, he will be satisfied with me. Yes, it is a wounded heart, a bleeding heart, that I offer him; but still a heart that is devoted and faithful.

August 25th.

I was certainly inspired. I do not wish, surely, to deceive myself. I am not happy; I can never be happy hereafter. I have felt a happiness too great, too perfect, to obtain consolation for having lost it. But still the constant thralldom of this single thought has ceased; my life has again a purpose and a future; I have created a duty which will fill its void, which will occupy me, and even attract me. Surely it is an attractive task to relieve little by lit-

tle a desolate soul, to withdraw it from despair, to
return to it peace and smiling contentment, to lead
it back to submission, to happiness, to God.   These
are the cares to which I consecrate myself with a
tender interest, which will daily increase more and
more, as a mother's affection for a sick child; and it
will leave him who is the object of it, I hope, nothing to regret.

At present he sees, he understands, all that I
give him, and with what sincerity I bestow it all.
I tell him something of it; he divines the rest, and
he seems happy.   As I imagined, our treaty no
longer holds good; he insists, it is true, that I shall
observe the delay arranged; I do not resist, but I
remain, and he does not complain.   I fancy we shall
be married in a few weeks.

It was necessary to confide this great secret to
Cécile and her *fiancé.*   I learned nothing from M.
d'Éblis, I believe; he said to me simply, "It is
worthy of you."   As for·Cécile, after a few seconds
of complete stupefaction, she went into a sort of fit
of joy and tenderness, which still lasts.   We shall
be cousins, almost sisters: it was her dream.   And
then she fancies that this marriage will rivet our

intimacy still more firmly, and that our separate existences will become, so to speak, commingled. Herein she is mistaken; she will remain the dearest of my friends; but it is likely that we shall live, for some time at least, more apart than hitherto. Until now, discouragement has prevented M. de Louvercy from yielding to the advice of his physicians, who prescribe for him a southern journey and the sea-side. But now he wants to live. I have already spoken of an establishment at Nice for the winter, and I have seen that he thanks me for more than one reason, perhaps.

Here I close my locked diary, never to reopen it, I trust. I believe that, once married, a woman should have no confidant but her husband. Adieu, then, romantic and impulsive Charlotte!

PART SECOND.

The extraordinary circumstances in which I find myself after the lapse of five years induce me to continue my journal. I am passing through a terrible ordeal: there has never been more necessity for order in my thoughts and conscience. In the first place, I want to recall to my mind the principal events which have led up to my present position, and try and draw from them the light and counsel of which I stand so much in need. And then, too, I have a presentiment that these pages will one day be read by some one besides myself, which is an added reason for my wishing that there should be no obscurity in them.

My marriage, as I had foreseen, took place at the same time as Cécile's, in the little church of Louvercy. M. and Mme. d'Éblis set out the next day for Italy, where they were to travel for several months.

Five or six weeks later I started myself for Nice, with my husband and my mother-in-law. My husband's health gave me the only serious solicitude that I knew for nearly four years, during which we lived in that charming climate. I cannot say that my heart was always free from regrets, from melancholy memories; but I can say that God really blessed the Quixotism of my marriage, and that it contained for me all that I had promised myself from it. It is untrue that the pleasures of passion take but one form, as we are too apt to think. There is some happiness in passion under the form of duty, devotion, and sacrifice; there is some, they say, in martyrdom itself. There was no question of martyrdom in my case, be it understood; but still a task like that which I had set myself has some difficulties and some drawbacks; it requires more than a day for the tenderest and best-loved hand to conquer and heal a soul that is naturally violent and made more so by misfortune. But then what an almost holy joy there is in fighting for this soul against revolt and doubt, and of discovering little by little that, beneath the ruins of the body, where it lies enshrouded, it is wholly pure! For some discouraged tears that I have shed in secret, how many were the sweet, happy, grateful ones that came to me as I felt my efforts rewarded! And at last the time came when I had but to raise my finger with a smile to see one of those frightful fits of anger, to which my poor Roger had formed the habit of abandoning himself, appeased at once.

I ought to add, lest I may boast too much, that the honor of this miracle was not due to me alone; it dated from the birth of my daughter, for which event her father forgave our heavenly Father.

It was just before her birth that Cécile and her husband, on their return from Rome, came to pass a few days with us at the villa of Palms, where we were living. I had secretly dreaded the moment when I should see M. d'Éblis again; but the great event in store for me rendered me almost indifferent to his presence, or at least I believed myself to be so. Besides, he was so icily ceremonious toward me that I was tormented with the idea that he had some grief to charge me with. Was he discontented with Cécile, and did he reproach me for having drawn too flattering a portrait when he consulted me? Certain new shades in his bearing toward his wife surprised me; he no longer appeared to be under the spell of her charm. Although he was always extremely courteous, there was a somewhat dry irony in his tone in speaking to her. At times he seemed wearied by the fantastic accounts which she gave us of her travels, her often intentional confusion of names, things, and dates, her impish assumption of erudition, and her pretty, bird-like prattle. But M. de Louvercy, to whom I spoke of my anxieties, assured me that the Commandant d'Éblis was, on the contrary, more in love with his wife than ever; that he was a little alarmed, perhaps, at seeing her so brilliant and sparkling, and so much admired, but that that was all. I thought no more of it then. I was too happy and too much occupied with my approaching maternity to think much of anything else.

Our plans were made to leave Nice at the end of spring, and return to Louvercy for the summer; my husband rejected absolutely all idea of an establishment at Paris. But the physicians were afraid of a sojourn in the country, and particularly in the damp climate of Normandy. Upon their advice, we decided to remain in the south until his health should become more settled. The two years which followed

brought me almost perfect serenity. My dear grandmother paid us two or three visits; my mother-in-
law evinced a passionate tenderness for me; then,
too, I had my daughter, and her birth, as I have
said, had reconciled my husband to life, and had attached him even more warmly to me. He was filled
with ardor for his work, in which I humbly seconded
him in the capacity of secretary, classifying, to the
best of my ability, the documents with which M.
d'Éblis kept us well supplied, making extracts, and
copying, in my daintiest handwriting, his illegible
fly-tracks. The active and earnest friendship which
he had inspired in M. d'Éblis was no longer a mystery to me, as I confess it had been before, when he
had allowed only his faults to be seen; but, since he
had ceased to fancy himself condemned to an isolated
existence, without affection or prospects, his great
qualities of mind and heart had appeared in all their
lustre and all their captivating charm. He had even
assumed a gayety which, in the beginning of our
acquaintance, I had been far from suspecting in
him. It was sweet to me to think that I had played
an intimate part in all these metamorphoses.

But what touched me more than anything else

was the absolute confidence he had in me. When
I married him, I had said to myself that all worldly life was ended for me, and I had honestly resolved to renounce it; it could not be agreeable to
me to seek pleasures that my husband could not
share. But he insisted that I should accompany his
mother to some of the *réunions* of the French and
foreign colony which was gayly whirling around us.
I did not abuse his permission; but I was happy to
profit by it occasionally in order that I might receive sometimes at my own house. I was naturally
exposed on the part of some of our guests and neighbors to those gallantries that are addressed to every
woman gifted with a passable exterior or a skillful
dressmaker. An infirm and ailing husband might
seem to offer an encouragement to these overtures;
but I met them with that tranquil reserve by which
it is always easy for a woman to make it understood
that she is not to be trifled with. My husband, with
his delicate insight and subtile appreciation, spoke to
me laughingly of these annoyances; he took pride,
I think, in showing me by his sovereign indifference
how high was the position I held in his esteem above
the shadow of a suspicion. I perfectly appreciated

it in him, but his confidence seemed to me excessive, for it plunged me into a somewhat serious embarrassment, which is unhappily connected with the greatest grief of my life.

There was, then, as there always is, at Nice a mixed society in which it was necessary to make distinctions. I am naturally a little exclusive, and I do not lend myself willingly to certain conciliations which have become a little too fashionable in these latter days. M. de Louvercy, like all his sex, I think, was more tolerant and liberal than I in these matters. He pretended that my *salon* was a fold into which I admitted only sheep that were without blemish and incapable of going astray; that it was dull, lacked sparkle, and, what is more, lacked charity, for it was discouraging to sinners of both sexes, and calculated to drive them to final impenitence, to shut the doors of honest houses against them, where they might learn to amend their ways through the general good atmosphere and example. To all his arguments I was quite insensible; I replied gayly that I had no mission to regenerate society, that having reformed him I had done enough for the edification of my life, and that I asked for nothing more.

In the spring of the third year of our sojourn in Nice, the young Prince Viviane came to live in the villa next to us. He brought with him a grand stud of horses, and a lady who was English, they said; and she must have been, if one could judge by the prismatic splendor of her toilets. Although my grandmother was connected with the dowager-princess, I do not remember ever to have seen the son, who led a not very creditable life, sometimes at Paris, but oftener at the various watering-places. He had hardly arrived when our colony was scandalized by his unrestrained dissipations, his reckless gambling, and his equivocal household. My husband, who had been one of his college friends, and who still felt a sort of affection for him, was nevertheless annoyed at his arrival, and especially at his proximity. However, it so happened that during the first of his stay at Nice we did not meet him.

I was walking one morning with my daughter and her nurse in the garden of our villa, in which were terraces communicating with each other by long marble steps. The lowest of these terraces looked out upon the public road, which was reached by a

final flight of about a dozen steps, with an iron gate
at the foot, which stood open during the day. We
were leaning on the railing and looking out at the
white waves of the sea, which seemed to have a
fascination for my daughter. The noise of approaching horses drew our attention to the road, and
we saw a few steps off a horseman accompanied by
a lady in a very elaborate and very ugly riding-
habit. As one of her many adornments, she wore
a magnificent white feather, curled around her rid-
ing-hat. She seemed to me, nevertheless, very beautiful. Just as this couple passed our garden, my
little girl was seized with great excitement, which
speedily degenerated into frenzy; she stretched out
her hands, screaming with all her might, while the
nurse, who was an Italian, sang to her all her most
soothing repertory. This concert caused the horseman to raise his eyes; he saw me, looked fixedly at
me, and raised his hat. Then, reining in his horse,
" What is the matter with your baby, nurse?" cried
he, laughing. Greatly surprised at this familiarity,
I drew back a little and told the nurse not to reply.
The woman did not understand, and coolly engaged
in a dialogue with the horseman over the wall. " I

think," she ended by saying, " the little one wants madame's white feather." " Give her your feather, Sarah," said the young man, turning toward his companion, who immediately took the feather out of her hat and threw it in the direction of the terrace. But the feather being too light fell down. The young man caught it on the fly, and threw it again with more force but with no greater success. " Oh, well," said he, very loud, " I am going to take it to the little thing myself." At the same instant the clink of the horse's hoofs sounded on the marble steps ; the animal slipped, fell back, and shivered with fright. I heard all this from behind the dense orange-trees where I had taken refuge, and I was wondering in some terror what this escapade could be, when suddenly I saw him appear upon the smooth grass of the terrace like an equestrian statue and advance triumphantly toward us. He bowed again to me, this time profoundly, and leaned over to place the feather in the hands of the child, whom this sudden vision had already appeased. Then, raising his hat for the third time, he descended the steps on his horse, I do not know how. When I related this adventure to my husband, a few min-

utes after, he said: "That must be Viviane; it is
exactly his way."

It was he, in fact. The same evening he presented himself at our house, giving as an excuse his
old relations with M. de Louvercy. I saw a tall,
fair-haired young man, very thin, with bold eyes,
delicate, beautiful features, and a bored expression,
a face of the court of the Valois. He laughed readily, and was very witty. My husband received him
with much cordiality. I was more reserved myself,
and hardly thanked him for the trouble he had
taken about the feather, not knowing exactly whether his politeness was addressed to my daughter, the
nurse, or myself.

This visit was followed by many others at short
intervals. I felt that his vivacity, and keen though
often absurd humor, amused my husband; still
I could not bring myself to attract or to retain
him. The prince had quite too much penetration
and knowledge of the world not to perceive the icy
reserve which I always manifested toward him; and,
in spite of his perfect self-possession, he seemed
sometimes disconcerted. My husband noticed this,
and even allowed it to annoy him. "My dear

child," he said to me one day as the prince was leaving us, "Viviane is going away quite crushed. When it suits you, you can really treat people in the most petrifying manner imaginable. Tell me, what has this poor fellow done to you?"

"Nothing, dear."

"No? Does he bore you, then? Is he too good-natured? He amuses me, you know; but I will receive him less amicably, to spare you the least annoyance."

"I assure you," I replied, "that there is absolutely nothing. I have never met the prince outside of my own drawing-room, and there, you know, he is propriety itself."

"Well, then, my dear, permit me to say that you are not—you treat him with an indifference that is really wounding."

"But, my dear, if I should encourage him ever so little, the first thing we know he will be bringing that young woman who is at his house."

"Oh, no! That is not a serious affair."

"It may not be; but what would you have? I hate disorder in all its forms. You know I cannot bear to see a piece of furniture out of place; and

for the same reason I cannot endure a man out of
the line of right and honor. For my part, I haven't
at all the weakness for fast men which they generally attribute to my sex ; and, besides, this one has a
special claim to the antipathy which I cannot avoid
showing. You are not ignorant of the connection
between his mother and my grandmother ; I have
been a witness more than once to the tears and despair of the poor princess on the subject of her son ;
and for a long time he has occupied a place in my
imagination and esteem which his actual conduct,
you must confess, is not of a nature to cause him to
forfeit."

"That is all very well, my dear, but as for the
poor princess, I would dispense with my pity for
her ; it was she who ruined her son by idolizing
him on bended knee, and persuading him that
heaven and earth were created for his particular
amusement. I remember that she once bought for
him a carriage and the goats at the Champs-Élysées.
The result is that he is going to marry, so they say,
this actress from Drury Lane. Well, it is logical."

"It is logical, my dear, but it is very unpleas-
ant."

It was a week before we again saw the prince at our house. He came at last one morning and shut himself up with M. de Louvercy. They had a long conference, of which my husband afterward gave me an account. M. de Viviane, it appeared, excused himself for having stopped his visits, by alleging, with a sort of melancholy, that he had felt they were not agreeable to me. My husband, touched by his serious and mortified tone, replied to him confidentially that he ought not to be surprised that his somewhat unconventional life should be a trifle startling to a young woman brought up under the strictest principles; that it depended entirely upon himself, moreover, to dissipate the unfavorable opinions which seemed to affect him so much, and that his friends of both sexes would gladly make their relations with him more easy and intimate.

"I am generally very indifferent to the opinion of the world," said the prince, "but I confess it has been hard for me to endure the contempt of Mme. de Louvercy."

"There is no question of contempt, my dear fellow," said my husband; "it is only the embarrassment of the thing." Thereupon they separated, the prince very pensive.

Two days after, on my return from a walk, my husband told me that M. de Viviane had just gone away. "I have asked him to dine with us to-morrow," added he. I opened my eyes wide; he began to laugh, and said: "He has sent the Englishwoman away, and invited his mother to come. That deserves some reward!" I agreed; and, when the prince came next day, I extended my hand with more warmth than had been my custom. We became better friends from that day, and he was unreservedly admitted into my circle.

However, as if to recompense himself, he had thrown himself furiously into play; he generally lost, which did him honor. At the same time, he told me one evening that he had just won about thirty thousand francs at baccarat. "You are truly a terrible man," replied I, shrugging my shoulders. "When one raises you on one side, you fall on the other!" At that, he drew from his pocket a great roll of bank-bills, and presented them to me.

"For your poor," said he.

"I accept," said I, "on one condition; that is,

that you give me your word never to touch a card
again."

" I give it to you."

And that is how I was enabled to send thirty
thousand francs to my grandmother for her young
apprentices' charity.

Finally—for he had a very complete assortment
of vices—he presented himself at our house a little
elevated, not to say intoxicated. There is nothing
in the world of which I have so great a horror as a
man in this state, and I wonder at the women—there
are very many of them, alas !—who think the thing
a joke, or who do not even notice it. The prince
could not fail to appreciate the sentiments which he
inspired in me on such occasions as this. He tried
to control himself, and became reasonably sober.
And thus he crowned that series of reformations,
accomplished through my entreaties, and seemingly
dedicated to me. These little triumphs, which di-
verted my husband (he laughed to see the prince
modestly holding worsted at my feet) did not fail to
interest and flatter me also ; but at the same time
they alarmed me a little. I thought over all these
sacrifices, asking myself if he did not expect some

compensation for them. These vague apprehensions continued to keep me on the defensive with him, and this did not escape his notice. We were walking one evening on one of the terraces; the beauty of the night, the almost suffocating odor of the orange-trees and violets with which the air was charged, had the effect of raising his discourse to the most poetic and sentimental heights. As I recalled him to earth rather dryly, " Great Heavens! madame," said he, " I do not know what more I can do to disarm your suspicions. To please you, I have thrown all my faults into the sea, one after the other. I have deprived myself of everything; I play no more, I drink no more, etc. What do you wish now? Shall I turn monk to please you? Tell me!" "I wish only one thing more," I replied, simply; "that is, that you should never make me question your friendship for my husband." He bowed very respectfully, and from that moment every equivocal shade disappeared from his language.

It was about this time that Cécile and her husband came to see us at Nice for the second time. My correspondence with Cécile had not ceased to be very frequent. To judge by her letters she was happy, although she seemed to seek her principal pleasures in worldly life. I found her more beautiful and very charming, but in no way modified by her marriage, and as volatile as ever. There was a constraint in her attitude toward her husband which struck me forcibly. As for him, he seemed very gentle toward her, but very reserved. I was astonished and almost frightened this second time to feel how much he had retained his influence over me, in spite of the time which had elapsed. I could not hear the sound of his voice without being deeply moved. He had not been twenty-four hours with us when I sought some means of abridging his stay. He furnished it himself by a very ill-advised indiscretion, which I have explained to myself since, but which at the time seemed perfectly incomprehensible.

Had my husband discovered in his heart some secret warning of what was passing in mine? Or did he feel the first approaches of the cruel malady which threatened him? I know not; but after the first days which followed the arrival of M. and Mme. d'Éblis he grew very gloomy. One morning M. d'Éblis asked me, in a tone of embarrassment, if I

had remarked this alteration in Roger's character.
Upon my replying in the affirmative, he permitted
himself, half laughing and half seriously, to allude
to the assiduities of the Prince de Viviane toward
me, allowing it to be understood that they might
awaken the susceptibilities of my husband. I knew
that M. de Louvercy was perfectly at ease, and
that he was even too much so, on the score of the
prince. I was certain, therefore, that the Commandant d'Éblis was not in this instance his inter-
preter, and that he was speaking on his own account.
That annoyed me beyond expression. I am not a
saint. I had pardoned him as well as I could for
having preferred Cécile to myself, and for having
married her after making love to me ; but that he
should pretend, after all that, to arrogate to himself
the right of conjugal surveillance over me, was a
little too much. "My dear sir," said I to him,
"since you have the kindness to interest yourself in
the secrets of my fireside, and in my domestic peace,
I would say to you that you are at the same time
right and wrong in your suppositions. You are
right, I believe, to attribute the moodiness of my
husband to a slight feeling of jealousy, but you are

absolutely mistaken as to the object." At these
words he became very pale, bowed, and left me.
Two days after he announced to us that he had been
called back to Paris, and he set out the same evening, leaving his wife with us.

I remember that the day after his departure
Cécile suddenly asked me a singular question. " Do
you believe," said she, " that my husband is happy ? "

" Surely, my dear, you ought to know better
than I."

" I fear," replied she, shaking her pretty little
head—" I fear that he is not ; I am too frivolous,
too worldly, too much carried away by pleasure. I
drag him after me like a martyr, poor man ! I reproach myself for it, and I continue. It is always
the demon which is in me, you know. He has not
complained ? He has not told you that he was unhappy ? Truly ? "

I told her with truth that I had received no confidences from M. d'Éblis, and she speedily resumed
her good-humor. She remained with us about a
fortnight ; and, though my friendship for her was
still as active and as tender as ever, I did not see
her depart without relief. Even perfectly honest a

7

woman as she was, she was too brilliant to be easily
protected.   The five parts of the world, which have
their representatives at Nice, buzzed around in
swarms, and my husband pretended that he would
have to put her night and day under guard.   Very
blasé with all this kind of homage, she still liked
it, and felt a little ill-will toward those who refused
it to her.   So it was that she was piqued by the
marked indifference shown her by Prince de Viviane.   She said that I had made a dunce of him, and
that I would have to lead him about with a rose-
colored ribbon.

Alas! all gayety went with her.   Some weeks
after her departure, my husband's health, which
seemed to have become more settled, altered mate-
rially; the most frightful and aggravating symptoms
succeeded each other.   The remainder of his poor
life was nothing more than an agony for him and
for me, and toward the end of the following winter
I had the terrible grief of losing him.   After so
much severe suffering he died very calmly, thanking me for having given him a few happy years.
M. d'Éblis, who had come to help him in his last
anguish, mourned him despairingly.   I pass briefly

over these bitter memories : God knows that the
expression of my grief, violent as it was, did not
lack sincerity, but at the time at which I write, it
would be wanting in propriety.

.   .   .   .

I passed the first months of my mourning with
my mother-in-law, and then I came to Paris to live
with my grandmother, expecting henceforth to di-
vide my existence between these two dear relatives.

Great moral agitations, like that which had come
to me, seem at first to suspend life ; our tastes, our
feelings, our passions, are dumb, as if stupefied by
the blow, and one fancies them dead.   Little by
little the heart begins to beat, the mind to think,
and it is at first almost an added grief—this im-
portunate persistence of life.   Then one reconciles
one's self to it, for God has willed it so.

In my new existence my daughter naturally held
the first place ; but this interest, great as it was, did
not absorb my whole heart.   I had again found dear
friends at Paris, and among the dearest and most
faithful were Cécile and her husband.   I saw Cécile
almost every day ; she recounted to me, with her
sparkling animation, the current stories of the city

and the world at large; she enlivened my solitude, she lavished the tenderest attentions upon me, and my affection for her returned in all its strength. I saw her husband more rarely; but he neglected no opportunity to be useful or agreeable to me. In the grievous trials through which I had passed, in the midst of the sad details which always accompany such events, and the painful questions of business which must be attended to, he showed a fraternal devotion for and assistance to me. The will of M. de Louvercy had made him the guardian of my daughter, and he seemed to have transferred to her the only passionate sentiment of his life—the heroic friendship he had felt for her father. It is needless to say that I had completely pardoned the strange indiscretion which he had committed in relation to Prince de Viviane. He remembered it himself only to seek to repair it by treating the prince with a particularly good grace wherever he met him, and especially at my house. For M. de Viviane was living then at Paris, and I received him often and familiarly, having had only perfect satisfaction to feel with him during the last months of my stay at Nice.

The only grief which M. d'Éblis caused me he did involuntarily and unconsciously. I could only reproach myself for the restless kind of pleasure with which I awaited his visits, and the secret emotion by which I felt agitated in his presence. But I hoped sincerely that this unfortunate remnant of my old attachment would vanish little by little, and finally lose itself in the round of daily habits. I hoped so all the more as his respectful courtesy and his cold and grave manner toward me were calculated to calm my heart rather than trouble it.

However, I occupied myself with extreme, and as I thought then, purely affectionate solicitude, with his attitude toward Cécile and the state of their relations, and the turn their marriage had taken. Nothing appeared to me more singular and more mysterious than their position toward each other and their mutual bearing. As I had noticed at Nice from several clear intimations, it was Cécile who, contrary to all logic, appeared to have usurped the sceptre in this household. She had seized the authority which the intellectual and moral superiority of her husband ought so naturally to have exercised, and M. d'Éblis, to all appearances, did not suffer from it. He submitted to the worldly and dissipated tastes of his young wife with an indifference and resignation that were inexplicable. After having for a long time accompanied her into society which he did not enjoy, he commenced to allow her to go alone. All this surprised me much. I asked myself what passed between them in their private life, whether they loved each other, whether they were happy. Not being able to question either of them upon points so delicate, I studied curiously, almost with avidity, their language, their conduct, the expression of their faces, their manner toward each other, in order to throw some light on the matter. But M. d'Éblis, with his severe grace, had an impassibility, sometimes grave, sometimes smiling like a sphinx, and Cécile was equally baffling in her very frivolity.

The world, like myself, was astonished at the peculiarities which this household offered, and had even begun to talk of them. One day the Commandant d'Éblis was at my house when Prince de Viviane arrived. M. d'Éblis, following his custom, sometimes a trifle too polite, withdrew almost immediately, after having exchanged a few friendly words with the prince. When he had gone: " Your cousin, there," said M. de Viviane, pleases me infinitely, but he is a veritable enigma to me."

" Why, an enigma ? "

" Because, with all the goodness and all the honor in the world, he seems to have sworn to allow his charming wife to be ruined."

" I really do not understand you."

" What! Don't you see that he leaves her to herself more and more ?   He does even worse than leaving her to herself, as he allows her to take Mme. Godfrey for a chaperon."

" Who is this Mme. Godfrey ? "

" Mme. Godfrey, madame, was formerly a very beautiful and much-courted woman, to say no worse of her; to-day she is one of those stars that are in their declension, and which, being unable to pretend to direct homage, manage to receive it in reflection by surrounding themselves with young satellites, and profiting by their reflection."

" I thank you for this information," said I, " and, if Mme. Godfrey is in fact a dangerous companion, be sure that Cécile will at once break off her relations with her.   For the rest, I am going to explain to you in one word what appears so inexplicable in the conduct of M. d'Éblis. M. d'Éblis has confidence in his wife, and permit me to assure you that confidence was never better placed. I have known Cécile from childhood, and with all her apparent giddiness, with or without Mme. Godfrey, I affirm that she is incapable of a wrong thought."

"Oh, of course! Yes, hitherto, certainly!" replied the prince. "All women begin by being honest; but, when they lead this kind of a life, wrong thoughts come quickly, and wrong actions even more quickly. It is very inconsistent, but it is true."

"Prince, these are your old man's memories of the time when you doubted if there were any upright women in the world."

"On my honor, now as always, I believe there are a few. Pardon me! Allow me! I am speaking only of the worldly ones, the excited and giddy ones who do not stop to take breath. Well, madame, will you credit my experience, which is quite considerable for its age? You have a daughter. Being born of you and educated by you, she can only be a good woman. Believe me, however, never

have the weakness to allow her to become passion-
ately fond of the world, at least not absorbingly. I
am going to tell you some horrible things, but we
men have one maxim which has become an axiom;
it is that a woman, however honest she may be,
ceases to be so after a heated carnival, or even—
you will shudder—after three or four hours of a
cotillion. Then arises a physiological phenomenon
which I confine myself to merely indicating to you;
but in short, it is no longer a woman that we hold
in our arms, no longer a thinking and conscious
being; it is no longer anything but—how shall I
tell you?—a sensitive plant ready to droop and fade
at the slightest touch."

I did not attach any undue importance to these
impertinent theories; but the language of the prince,
without leaving in my mind any doubt of Cécile,
did not the less confirm my personal observations of
the mysterious and troubled character of her household.

A circumstance which immediately followed my
conversation with M. de Viviane will serve to explain what I mean: Cécile and her husband were
dining with me one day; Cécile, who was looking

her best and in a dazzling toilet, was going to a ball in the evening with Mme. Godfrey, who called for her at half-past nine. My grandmother, being a little indisposed, kept her room, so that my daughter and I were left alone with M. d'Éblis. My daughter ought to have been in bed; but, as with all children, a great deal of urging was required to accomplish this ceremony, and, at the request of her guardian, I had granted her a reprieve. Immediately after Cécile's departure, feeling a little embarrassed by this sort of *tête-à-tête* with M. d'Éblis, I seated myself at the piano: M. d'Éblis sat upon a sofa at the other end of the *salon*, and, while playing some one of Chopin's melodies, I heard him talking in low tones with my daughter, whom he petted a great deal, and whose very great friend he was. After a little while they both became silent; I had a mirror before me, and, raising my eyes to it, I saw M. d'Éblis leaning on the table, his forehead on his hand. A minute after, my daughter, who had approached me with hesitating steps, pulled me gently by the sleeve; I leaned a little to one side without stopping my playing, and the child whispered in my ear, "Mamma, he is crying!" At this confidence of the poor little one, a sort of languid intoxication diffused itself throughout my veins, and my whole being. These are momentous seconds in the life of a woman.

The door opened; the nurse came after my daughter. I kissed her, she went to kiss M. d'Éblis, and retired.

I continued to play without daring to raise my eyes to the glass, and I tried to collect my thoughts and understand clearly what was passing. The sudden emotion of M. d'Éblis in the presence of my daughter and me, after the departure of his wife, left me no doubt that he was profoundly unhappy. Anything more I could not get even a glimpse of. But, if I could not read his heart, I read my own clearly, and what I discovered there frightened me. I could no longer deceive myself as to the kind of interest that induced me to study Cécile's domestic secrets so curiously. I loved her husband, and I loved him enough to desire the disruption of his household, and to rejoice in it.

A thousand times in my life I have observed that it does not depend on ourselves to experience or not to experience criminal feelings, but that it does always depend upon ourselves not to allow them to pass into actions. I have observed, further, that the best and perhaps the only means of combating and conquering evil passions is not to oppose to them abstract arguments of reason, conscience, or honor, but to act against them effectively, and in a manner to force the hand to do good when the heart desires evil.

My resolution taken, I wanted to execute it without delay.

It required, first of all, a frank and complete explanation with M. d'Éblis. This was a trial whose dangers I did not disguise from myself, although I was far from foreseeing all their gravity. But it seemed to me necessary to bear them; and, in the excitement of my enthusiasm, I believed myself certain of conquering them.

I left the piano suddenly and approached M. d'Éblis, who pretended to be attentively reading. "I want to speak with you," said I to him; "come into the garden, please."

He looked at me with an air of extreme astonishment, rose without replying, and followed me.

Our hotel in the Rue St. Dominique, by rare

good fortune, preserved its secular garden, to which
an environment of high walls, groups of gigantic
palms, a bubbling fountain, and a vaulted green-
house, lent the sweet and solemn aspect of the yard
of a Spanish cloister. The *salon* on the ground-
floor is approached by two or three steps. Although
it was then the middle of November, the evening
was exceptionally serene and mild. We took a few
steps in silence. I still hear, and I shall hear all
my life, that silence, broken only by the rustle of the
dry leaves under our feet and the murmur of the
little fountain.

At last, summoning all my courage, "Monsieur,"
said I to him, "you know to what extent I carry
my love for order and my dislike to disorder; it is
a passion, a mania about which you have often teased
me, but which you pardon in me, do you not?
Well, will you permit me to reëstablish order in a
household in which I am much interested?"

"In what household, madame?" said he, quite
severely, taking his place beside me on the bench
where I had seated myself.

"In what but yours, naturally? I am sensible
—do not doubt it—of the extent of my indiscre-

tion ; but, if my friendship for Cécile and for you does not suffice to excuse it in your eyes, remember that you were good enough to ask my advice before marrying Cécile, that I advised that union, and allow me to discharge my responsibility."

" But, madame, I reproach you with nothing."

" And you are right ; that would be very unjust, for, if you had followed the advice that I allowed myself to give you—at your own entreaty, moreover—you would both be happy; and you are not, either of you."

· " Pardon me, madame, but it seems to me that Cécile at least, whom I allow the most entire freedom, should be perfectly happy."

" Cécile does not complain," said I, with some warmth ; " but to suppose that she can be perfectly happy when you live your life and she hers, when you neglect her, when you intrust her to the first comer, when you prove to her more and more that you care neither for her affection nor even for her reputation, is to suppose that she has no intelligence, nor heart, nor honor—and I know that she has them all ! "

" Good Heavens, madame ! " he returned, in a

constrained voice, that was nevertheless moved and unsteady, "neither am I accustomed to complain, but really you force me to it. Tell me, have you ever thought of the fate of a man occupied with serious thoughts, loving work, and ambitious of the honor that it brings, who has dreamed of the joys of study in the charm and retirement of his fireside, and whom his wife drags after her day and night into the noisy emptiness and perpetual whirl of fashionable life? It is very well to feel that duty, and even prudence, demands that he should follow her —when he sees at last that her whole life is passed there—that this child, this simpleton to whom he is bound, robs him, degrades him, destroys his intelligence, his future, his dignity, his life—what would you have then?—he loses heart, he gives up, discouraged in everything, and utterly resigned!"

Surprised and almost frightened by this violent outburst from a soul habitually so much the master of itself, I said to him, more gently: "But come, monsieur, frankly, have you in all sincerity made every effort to reform Cécile's tastes?"

After a long pause, "I have made none," he said, coldly.

"Surely, then, you are much to blame. I told you once, and I repeat it to-day with the same conviction, with the same certainty : Cécile was a spoiled child, but her faults were only superficial ; she loved and respected you ; you had entire control over her, and there were no sacrifices that you could not have obtained from her ! "

" And by what right could I have demanded them of her ? " resumed M. d'Éblis. " My conscience was clear. What had I to give her in exchange for the pleasures that she might have sacrificed for me ? One asks such sacrifices only from the woman one loves ! "

" From the woman one loves ! Great Heavens ! do you speak of Cécile ? What ! when you married Cécile, you did not love her ! "

" Never ! " said he, with emphasis. Then he added, in a lower tone, very rapidly : " Oh ! I did not deceive her ; God is my witness ! I deceived only myself—and you ! "

At this the whole truth became clear to me. I rose in utter distraction. A cry escaped me : " Ah, unhappy man, what have you done ? "

" I have done," said he, " what you will understand better than any one else. I throw myself upon your mercy! O madame, I did not seek this conversation; I would have shunned it rather, for doubtless it will separate us forever. So be it! But, since we have come to it, my heart must unburden itself at last! You must know all. Let me finish, I beg of you! I am speaking to you, you see, with profound respect. Well! will you recall the past? When Roger revealed to me his fatal passion for you, when I understood that I must choose between you and him, that I could no longer love you without consigning him to despair—to suicide, perhaps —I sacrificed myself. And then, by a courageous effort—which I believed possible, which I believed sincere—I tried to transfer my love to that child, whom you loved, who was entirely enveloped by the reflection of your charm and your tenderness. Yes, I believed I loved her; but it was still you that I loved in her. And, though this word must be the last I shall pronounce before you, to-day, as then, it is you only, you of all the world, whom I love!"

I heard all this in a stupor, my eyes fixed on the darkness. Suddenly, at the poignant thought of this lost happiness, my tears fell in spite of myself.

He leaned forward a little and saw my emotion. "You weep!" said he. "Is it true, then, is it possible? You also—you love me?—you have suffered like me? Great God, do not tell me so! Do not let me think it, if you do not wish to make me lose all sense of right and honor that is left me!"

My hand rested gently on his arm, and I said to him: "It is not I, monsieur, I hope, who would ever cause you to lose either reason or honor; but I loved you much—I love you still! If you are worthy to hear such an avowal from the lips of an honest woman, I am about to prove it. I cannot stifle the emotions of my heart, but I can at least—and I rely upon it that you can also—raise them high enough to purify them. We will not separate like two feeble creatures who are afraid of becoming the miserable sport of their passions. Let us guard our mutual affection bravely, and give it a new character—make of it an almost sacred tie, uniting us both in a generous copartnership to secure the best we know. You know already what task I had proposed to myself before I knew the truth. I hold to it now more than ever. Aid me loyally to accomplish it, aid me to reconquer for you the heart of your

wife; I promise you to help her conquer yours.
Will you? If you say yes, I esteem you so highly
that I shall place my hand in yours with absolute
confidence; otherwise—farewell!"

He reflected for a few seconds, then without
speaking he tendered me his hand. I rose immediately, and we returned to the *salon.* "You will
send Cécile to me to-morrow," I said to him; "I
wish to begin my preachments very gently. As for
you, I will not tell you to be indulgent with her;
you are too much so already. On the contrary,
scold her; I am sure she will be charmed to be
chided by you. It is indifference which alienates
us women!"

He bowed, walked off a few steps, and then
turning—"Good Heavens!" said he, "I forgot—
you know I leave to-morrow with the general for a
month or six weeks—an inspection in the provinces.
It is extremely annoying."

"Perhaps not," said I, "for during her widow-
hood Cécile will necessarily be more retired; it will
be a beginning. On your side, you will have time
for reflection, and on your return you will know
better if you are really capable of keeping the en-

gagement that you have just taken somewhat hastily, it seems to me, somewhat lightly—"

"No," said he, in his gentle and resolute voice, "not lightly. I understood you at once. My life was lost; your friendship raises it again and rescues it. What you propose to me is very lofty, very heroic, but you will carry me to it on your wings. Farewell, madame. Trust me." And he left me.

I passed a sleepless but happy night. I was satisfied with myself. I had conquered a great temptation. If ever a woman should read this, and if she has ever met in her life a man whom she had wished to press to her heart once though she should die in doing it, she will understand me.

The next afternoon Cécile came to me and told me that her husband had set out that morning for Brittany. "My dear," said she, "that frigid individual astonished me. He begged me to write to him every day. Can you fancy such an idea? I thought, however, it was mere absence of mind, and that he doesn't attach any importance to it. And he is right, for certainly I shall not write him every day."

"Why not?"

"Have I time? But it is absurd. I will send

him dispatches: 'Are you very well? I am! A thousand kisses! Cécile.' It will be quite sufficient."

" But tell me, Cécile, do you not intend to remain at home a little more during your husband's absence?"

" Remain at home? What do you wish me to do at home? Besides, what difference does it make? Whether my husband is present or absent, seems much the same thing so far as I can see!"

" Cécile, be serious a moment, I beg you, and let us talk this over."

" Yes, my angel."

" Don't you tire of this life a little?"

" No, my treasure!"

" Ah, well! I confess I am beginning to love you less."

She clasped me round the neck. " That is not true!"

I tried a while longer to draw her into an intimate and confidential conversation; she did not resist directly, but she constantly eluded it and escaped with some jest. I saw that my task would be more difficult than I had supposed, and that the dear child had acquired a terrible relish for her fatal manner of living. But I was still persuaded that I could, with a little perseverance, recapture this noble heart, whose essential virtues I knew so well.

She had already begun to defend herself, with rather more embarrassment, when Prince Viviane was announced, and she was evidently much relieved to have this pretext to escape me this time. She rose, threw a few sarcastic remarks at the prince—for she held a constant grudge against him for what she called his infatuation, that is to say his indifference toward her—then she went out. As I accompanied her into the antechamber—

"My lovely preacher," said she, laughingly, "I am going to take my revenge. You reproach me, or you would like to reproach me, with my manner of life, which is a little flighty, I confess; but, if you should consult my husband, I imagine that he would prefer to leave me in my whirlwind rather than see me seated at my fireside four or five times a week with such a man as that. What do you think?"

"What! Does M. d'Éblis disapprove of my receiving the prince?"

"Not exactly, but I really believe that he is jealous even now on account of his poor friend Roger, for he cannot endure your prince. And the fact is, my dear, that he comes here very often; I assure you it is talked about."

"Ah, well, my dear," said I, "I will prove to you that I can profit by good advice, and I hope that you will imitate my example."

"Yes, my love; I adore you!" and she ran away.

I rejoined the prince, meditating on that malicious insinuation of Cécile's. However, it only made me hasten to execute a resolution that I had already taken. For some time past the attentions of the prince had really become very frequent, and they began to annoy me. Nevertheless, his wit amused me, his language with me never forgot respect; finally, the improvement in his life had not changed since his return to Paris, and, as that improvement was in part my work, I tried to preserve it. So it could not enter my mind to give him a humiliating dismissal; I simply desired to divest our relations of the too intimate character that he more and more studied to give them.

In the course of our conversation, he himself furnished me with the opportunity I sought by asking me if I would be at home that evening. "Yes," said I, laughingly, "I shall be—but not to you!"

"Why not to me?"

"Because your time is too precious, prince, for me to abuse it so far."

"You have had enough of me?"

"I have not had enough of you—but I do not wish too much," I returned, in the same tone. "Come, you do not intend to compromise me, do you?"

"Ah! but I beg your pardon," said he, gayly.

"Still more reason, then. I have a friendship for you, but I shall really be obliged to receive you less frequently."

I was surprised at the serious expression that his features suddenly assumed.

"I must explain, then," said he. "I wished to wait a little time longer; but I see that the moment is come for it. It is true that I have multiplied my visits unscrupulously, because my feelings for you justified the indiscretion in my eyes. I love you, madame, and my love does not date from yesterday.

Pardon me! I know perfectly to whom I am speaking. I know that such an avowal addressed to such a woman as you has no two interpretations possible; for one to offer his heart to you is to offer you his name. You have made yourself mistress of my life; by your goodness you have made a new man of me—a better man. Will you be kind enough, charitable enough, to accomplish your work? May I hope that one day you will deign to be my wife?"

This unexpected proposal caused me more surprise and annoyance than uneasiness. Wishing to spare the prince the mortification of a too abrupt and too absolute a refusal, I said to him, hesitating a little, that I was sincerely grateful for so marked an evidence of esteem, but that he took me quite by surprise; that I could not complain of a proposal so unexpected, since I had in a measure provoked it in spite of myself, but that my bereavement was still too recent to permit me even to discuss it. I begged him, therefore, to speak of it to me no more.

While accepting the most extended delay that I could desire to impose upon him, he earnestly insisted upon obtaining a less vague answer—a word of hope. Honesty preventing me from giving him

8

this satisfaction, I was under the necessity of emphasizing my refusal. I said plainly to him, although with consideration and courtesy, that I had taken a firm resolution to devote myself to my daughter, and never to remarry.

There was doubtless some chagrin, but there was, above all, what seemed to me spite, anger, and wounded pride, in the countenance and accent of the prince, after I had made him this formal declaration. I again perceived in him, under the refined manner of the man of the world, the spoiled child whose caprices had always been laws, and who must have formerly broken the playthings that had been refused him. His pale and almost sallow countenance was painfully contracted; his eyelids opened and closed spasmodically, and his eyes shot out an evil light at me. I was going to make of him, he said to me in broken accents, a despairing man—a profligate! I was going to plunge him again into the slough which he had come out of to please me! At my age I could not seriously entertain the thought of remaining a widow; doubtless I was waiting for a better match. I would, perhaps, regret him one day; I would repent having refused him my hand. One became wicked when one was unhappy; and much more of the same sort, which seemed to me in deplorable taste. I observed with sadness that where vice has been there always remains a depth of mire. I was soon to appreciate this more fully.

Finally, he felt that he was insulting me, or rather that he was losing his own self-respect. He recollected himself, apologized, tried to turn his ravings into jest, and left me on good enough terms, begging me in spite of all to preserve my friendship for him. I promised it to him, but promised myself the contrary. For I had never had much confidence in him, and I had no longer any at all.

Five or six days passed. Surprised not to see Cécile again, for she was not accustomed to let so long an interval elapse between her visits, I decided to go to her house, without much hope of meeting her, for she lunched every day with some one or other. However, I found her, but it was in the company of Prince Viviane, who was seated opposite her at the fireside. On seeing him there, I could not resist a painful impression—an oppression of the heart. I knew that until that time the prince

had never set foot in Cécile's house, and that she
had even bitterly complained of it. This change of
habit annoyed me, and my annoyance was not les-
sened when I learned by some allusions that escaped
them that this visit had been preceded by another a
few days before, and, further, they were to meet the
same evening at Mme. Godfrey's, where they both
were to dine. It was impossible for me not to
establish a connection in my thoughts between these
unusual circumstances and the equivocal, almost
menacing words that the prince had left me for
adieux. He knew of my sisterly affection for Cécile ; had he formed a project of disturbing me at
least by transferring to my best friend the attentions
which I no longer desired, and avenging himself
upon her for my disdain ? However unworthy and
despicable such a design might be, I was not so ignorant of the world as to be unaware that the embit-
tered soul of a libertine was capable of conceiving
it. This man, it is true, in offering to marry me
had seemed to give token of some honest and serious feeling; but it was because he had found me
beautiful, and had seen no other means of becoming
master of my person.

I waited impatiently till he should go. Hardly was I alone with Cécile when I fell on my knees before her, and, kissing her hands, I said, " Let me speak to you—will you ? "

" Speak, golden mouth ! but speak quickly, for I must dress. You know I do not dine at home."

" Will you give me an immense pleasure, my dear ? Do not dress; send a word of regret to this Mme. Godfrey, who is not thought well of, by-the-way, and come and dine with your old, old friend."

" Ah, we are still at it ! " said Cécile, laughing, but a little awkwardly. " Well, then, let us exhaust the subject. I wish it very much. Upon my honor, what do you reproach me with ? Do I misconduct myself ? Come, do you believe that ? No, you do not believe it; you know that I am simply what I have always been—a little creature who has quicksilver in her veins, who loves movement, excitement, gayety, compliments, the dance—all the *tra la la* of life; but, in fine, an honest little creature who does no wrong—who is devoted to her friends and faithful to her husband ! What more is necessary for her ? "

" My dear little one, I do not blame you for loving pleasure; I blame you for loving only that. You had formerly—allow me to remind you—a more serious and true conception of life; in our girlish conversations we imagined something better than this endless dissipation, and this kind of intoxication in which you so strangely delight. We used to give a place, a great place, in our future existence to more intimate, more select, more worthy pleasures. Good Heavens! you do nothing wrong, to be sure, but you do nothing good. For example, you do nothing to elevate your tastes, your sentiments, your ideas; you develop yourself only in the direction of your weaknesses. Then, too, believe me, this continual lightness of conduct, of attitude, of language, is not without danger in the long-run; for all serious things in this world are bound together somehow. Honesty and virtue are grave things which need to rest upon a serious foundation of existence. They are scattered in the whirl and frivolity of a wholly exterior life. Little by little they lose the consistency and solidity which are essential to them, and without which they no longer have force enough to rule our passions. Thus a woman finds herself suddenly unarmed before the least temptation, the least excitement. In short, I beg you, my dear child, to stop where you are in this downward course, and let me add that the absence of your husband furnishes you with a very natural excuse, and that it even imposes it upon you as a duty!"

She listened to me, alas! in a kind of impatient abstraction, tapping the carpet with her little foot.

"Well, be it so!" she returned, "it is possible; "perhaps there is some truth in your sermon; I will think of it; but, as for this evening, I have formally promised Mme. Godfrey—and I shall go."

"No, I beg of you!"

"But, really, why this insistance? Why do you so particularly desire that I should not go to Mme. Godfrey's this evening? Be frank; it is on account of Prince Viviane, whom you were displeased to find with me!"

"Good Heavens! Very likely," said I.

"How very pleasing! You reserve him exclusively for yourself, it appears!"

"I reserve him for myself so little that I have refused his heart and hand which he wished to offer

me, one accompanying the other, five days ago. If
I betray this secret, it is because I feel myself almost forced to it to put you on your guard against a
man whom I believe to be infinitely dangerous. I
shall be at ease now; for, supposing that he intends
to make love to you—as he seems disposed to do—
you will be edified by the sincerity of the sentiments he will express for you. I know your delicacy and pride, and I know what reception a rejected lover who dares to ask consolation from you
may hope for."

She stood up in front of me, her eyes on the fire.

"I do not believe you," she cried—"I do not
believe a word that you have just said! Confess
the truth: you are jealous—that is it!"

"Cécile, is it you who are speaking?"

"Yes, it is I; and, I tell you, you are jealous!
What! for two years or more you have been accustomed to seeing the prince *tête-à-tête* every day, or
nearly every day—and that is quite natural—that is
perfectly proper—and, since he happens to come to
me twice, everything is upset! You are jealous!
Well, never mind, I will return you your prince.
I'm sure I don't keep him."

"Ah! my poor child, where have you learned that tone? Do you know, you offend me?"

"Indeed it is you who have offended me for the last hour; and you always have, by treating me like an unreasoning child, and a woman without honor! Never mind; good-evening. Leave me to get dressed!"

My eyes, half wild with grief and astonishment, sought hers, but in vain; she shunned my look. I took a few steps toward the door.

"Charlotte!" said she, "give me your hand!"

"No," said I, "you are not worthy of it." And I went out.

I returned home with a sore heart. In the first grief which followed this scene, it seemed to me that everything was leaving me, that everything was giving way. I was losing the dearest friendship of my life; at the same time I was losing the great interest which bound me to life again, and upon which I had counted to occupy and soothe my heart. I saw myself prevented by Cécile's obstinate waywardness from keeping the compact I had made with her husband. Henceforth, how should I ask his good-will and assistance toward a reconciliation to which his wife was hostile? How should I reveal the sad truth to him? How should I even see him again?

At this reflection, however, my agitation was a little calmed. I told myself that it was impossible that Cécile could be so changed and hardened as to have become an absolutely different person from herself. I remembered that she had formerly had these fits of ill-temper and anger with me, that she had always been sorry for them, and that her excellent heart had quickly got the better of them. I hoped that it would be the same in this instance, and that she would come to me the next day ashamed and repentant.

But I was not destined to pass the next day in Paris. Very early in the morning I received a letter from Mme. Hémery, Mme. de Louvercy's housekeeper, who announced that my mother-in-law was seriously ill; she wished to see me, and also her granddaughter. I forgot every other anxiety, and set out immediately with my daughter for Louvercy.

My mother-in-law had an attack of violent bronchitis, which had presented symptoms at first that had alarmed her physician. But the disease was quickly subdued, and a week after our arrival she was entirely out of danger. I greatly desired to return to Paris, but it was impossible. It was already December, and it had become my custom to take my daughter each year to her grandmother's for the Christmas holidays and New-Year's; and, as we were now so near them, I had no excuse for not prolonging my visit till then.

In the mean time there came a letter from Cécile which removed a part of my cares, but which left very many and very grave ones. Here is the letter, which will later play a great part in very unhappy circumstances:

" Cécile d'Éblis to Charlotte de Louvercy.

" My well-beloved Charlotte, I hastened to you on Monday like a poor, crazy person. The news of your departure has overwhelmed me. I had to return home with this mountain resting on my heart. Oh, my darling, tell me we are not enemies! When you refused me your hand the other evening, it seemed to me that my good angel had abandoned me, and that I fell, I knew not where. Oh, my dear Charlotte, I do not believe a word of those unworthy things I said to you. I beg your forgiveness for them on my knees. You were a thousand times right to blame my miserable mode of life; but don't you see that the bottom of it all is that I am unhappy, frightfully unhappy! My husband is an excellent man, full of merit and honor; but he has one terrible failing—he does not love me! I have felt it for a long time, almost since the first day, and it is killing me! He does not ill-treat me. He is indulgent to me, but it is an indulgence that freezes me. He does not love me! Ah, well! What would you have a woman do who perceives that? There is but one remedy—not to think, not to reflect, to fasten bells on one's head and feet, and divert one's self with the noise! And yet that does not always suffice; there are moments when heart fails me, when I almost lose my head, when I feel that I am on the point of some desperate act—of a last and irreparable folly! Can you not see if I have need of your love! As for me, I adore you.

Cécile."

This letter frightened me, not only by the disorder of mind which was stamped upon it, but above all by the strange insistance with which Cécile, for the first time, complained of her husband's faults, of which until then she had seemed so little sensible. One would have said that she had discovered them suddenly, as if she had taxed her wits to find griefs in order to create or prepare excuses.

I answered her at length the same day. I tried to calm her exaltation by assuring her, in the first place, that my tender friendship for her, though cooled for an instant, remained no less entire and unalterable on that account : then I tried to prove to her that her husband sinned toward her only by excess of complacency; that she could not seriously reproach him for not giving up his work, his career, his future, to take part in all his wife's pleasures; that she herself would be the first to blame him for it, and to suffer for it in her pride; that she would really be nearer right if she would accuse herself of want of affection, since he had made so many sacrifices for her, and she had made none for him : that perhaps—that certainly, even—in the secrecy of his heart, M. d'Éblis reproached her as she did him; that it, depended entirely upon her to break the ice

which had formed between them, and that I had
reason to believe that the least effort on her part
toward a reconciliation with her husband would be
met with gratitude and with effusion; that, besides,
I had determined to destroy this sad misunderstand-
ing between them, and, if she would only aid me a
little, the new year that was about to commence
would see happiness reseated at her fireside at the
same time that she should take her station there herself. I reminded her, in closing, that her husband
before his departure had asked her to write him almost every day, and I begged her to respond less
lightly than she had before to this request, which
cer‎ainly was not a mark of indifference.

A little reassured after having sent this letter, I
was still more so in receiving, a few days later, a
note from Cécile, rather short, but in which she
seemed to display a good deal of steadiness and wis-
dom. She thanked me very tenderly. She said
that I was right, and it was she who had spoiled her
happiness; but she had determined to repair her
fault; she awaited her husband's return, impatient
to begin her reformation at once; but she awaited
him also with some timidity, because her deep at-

tachment to him had always been alloyed with a little fear.

Spite of its being in singular contrast with the tone of her preceding letter, this language seemed natural and sincere to me; and, knowing that M. d'Éblis was to reach Paris the following week, I felt myself freed from all the unhappy apprehensions which I had brought to Louvercy.

On the evening of December 17th Mme. de Louvercy, my daughter, and I, had finished dinner, when we thought we heard a sound of bells and the cracking of a whip in the direction of the avenue. All of us listened with surprise, for we were living in great retirement; except the curé and the doctor, who came to us in the daytime, we received no one, and were still further from expecting a visit from a stranger, as the weather was extremely severe. It was freezing hard, and since the night before there had fallen a great quantity of snow, which buried us in our woods and separated us from the rest of the world. One's curiosity is easily aroused in the country. My daughter ran to the window. " It is a carriage," said she; " I see the lamps; they are coming—they are coming!" I got up also; I rubbed the frost off a pane with my handkerchief, and saw myself the black form of a carriage plowing through the snow-drifts and advancing slowly toward the château, skirting the frozen pond. Save the feeble tinkling of the bells no more was heard, the wheels sliding rather than rolling over the thick white carpet which covered the ground.

My mother-in-law and I were asking each other who it could be, when the door opened suddenly, and we could not repress a cry of astonishment at seeing Cécile enter. She came toward us with her abrupt and rapid step, embraced her aunt, then me, and said to us with a nervous laugh: "I wanted to give you a surprise. My husband writes that he is unable to return for a week; the idea occurred to me of passing that week with you—and here I am, only I was delayed on the road by this snow. We were more than three hours coming from the station; I am chilled, and shivering—" Indeed, she was shaking in all her limbs; I was struck at the same time with the pallor and the change in her features, which I attributed to the cold she had endured and the languor which followed it.

While her aunt was gently reproving her folly,

and thanking her for her thoughtful attention in the same breath, I made her sit down before the fire; then I gave orders to have dinner brought in for her. But she would take nothing; she had dined at Mantes, she told us. She began with feverish volubility to relate the incidents of her journey, the trouble she had had to find a carriage at the station, and the fright of her maid in the middle of the woods so full of snow. At times she interrupted herself, and sat still with her eyes fixed straight before her. Then she would hastily resume her narrative and her fits of childish laughter. Toward nine o'clock, Mme. de Louvercy, who was still ill, begged her to excuse her, and went up to her room. "You will do well," I said to Cécile, "to go to bed also; you look completely tired out; we will talk to-morrow as much as we like." "No, no," she answered, "I am recovered. Let us go to your room. We can chat there better than in the *salon.*"

My room was the same that I had occupied six years before during my first visit at Louvercy, in the angle tower of the château. I had preferred it to any other on account of the memories it called up for me. Besides, it adjoined that which my grandmother had had, and in which I had put my daughter. We went thither, Cécile and I, preceded by Mme. Hémery, the housekeeper, who carried a light. She turned up the wick and left us. She had scarcely gone when Cécile threw her hat on the bed and hastened to shut the double door which was half open. Then coming toward me with an automatic step, she fixed her eyes on mine with a terribly wild expression, placed her hands on my shoulder, and said in a low and dull tone which I shall never forget :

"Charlotte—I am ruined !"

A chill like death froze my veins. "My God !" I exclaimed in a hoarse whisper, "what are you saying to me ?"

"The truth," she replied in the same tone; "I am ruined !"

I remained for some seconds utterly overwhelmed —motionless, speechless; then with an inquiring look, "The prince ?" I said.

She bowed her head with a gesture of gloomy acquiescence.

"You are—?" I asked again, in a lower tone.

"Yes!—How?—Why?—I know not!—I yielded —without reason, without excuse, without passion, wretched girl that I was!"

I saw that she was fainting. I supported her and helped her to reach a sofa, on which she sank. I fell on my knees before her, and, holding my head in my hands, I wept bitterly.

Very soon I felt her fingers stroking my hair.

"Dear, good Charlotte," she murmured, "you are weeping for me! Ah, I was an upright woman before that, I swear it to you! And to think I can never again be one—never; that I have that stain on my forehead, that shame in my heart, for the rest of my life! Oh! is it true? Is it possible? Great God, what an awakening!—Ah, if they knew—if they only knew!"

"Oh, my poor, poor child!" I said to her, kissing her hands.

She drew them from me. "No! no!" she said, "I entreat you. I am no longer worthy; I am dishonored and detestable!—Ah, my God, have pity! Let me go mad, I pray thee!" and she clasped her uplifted hands convulsively.

"And now," cried she, suddenly starting up,

" what am I to do ?   I lied to you at first in telling
you that my husband would not be back for a week;
he returns to-morrow !—to-morrow, do you hear ?
That is why I fled—why I came to cast myself on
you, to ask you what I shall do.   I cannot see him
again—I cannot !   He was so good to me—so good
—and he is so honorable himself ! "

" Dearest, indeed you must see him again," I
said, through my tears.

" How can I ?   It is impossible, unless I confess
all to him !   Yes, I would like to tell him all ; whatever comes of it, whether he kills me or pardons
me, I shall be released, shall I not ?   I ought to
confess—you advise me to ? "

I made no reply.

" Then," said she, getting up, " I have only to
kill myself ! "

I forced her back gently and sat down beside
her.   " Compose yourself, let us be calm, my Cécile,
I pray you.   Let me think—let me reflect.   This is
all so sudden, so perplexing.   Let us see : you ask
me if you ought to confess your fault to your husband.   Good God, I hardly dare restrain you, for
surely it is a good impulse ; and yet I do not truly

think it would be wise. In the first place, there are offenses that men never pardon; and, then, your husband would seek vengeance. You would mention no names, I know very well; but he would find out; it would be very difficult to keep the truth from him; and you foresee what would happen then. Indeed, dearest, even supposing this danger averted, even supposing he pardons you, I think that confession of your fault would risk and even surely forfeit the little happiness that you two can still hope for."

"And what happiness, great God, do you think I can hope for or can give him with the secret of this sin between us?"

"You alone know of this fault, at least; and you, only, will suffer for it. It seems to me that sharing your grief and shame with your husband almost aggravates them, and that keeping all their bitterness to yourself is in itself some slight expiation."

"I could not," she whispered, shaking her head wearily.

Her beautiful hair fell in disordered waves over her shoulders, and half covered her forehead and her face ; her arms hung inert at her sides ; her dry eyes were fixed on vacancy with a frightful stare. She was such a heart-rending image of absolute despair, that anything which would raise her courage seemed to me justifiable. "Dearest," I said to her, holding her tightly against my heart, "you thought you were not loved; that is what ruined you. I would not too much extenuate your fault, which is very great, but you are not without excuse ; at least you thought you were not."

"Excuse," said she, bitterly ; "I have not the shadow of one ! "

"Reflect ; you wrote me not long ago that it was the indifference, the neglect of your husband, that had driven you into this giddy and dissipated life. Reflect ! "

"I lied," she said, in a dull tone ; "you know it very well. It was I who disheartened my husband ; it was I who neglected him, who preferred my senseless pleasures to his affection, and to happiness, and to honor! That is the truth! You predicted yourself whither it would all lead me. No, I have no excuse, not one."

"Well, in spite of all, nothing should be de-

spaired of. Come, do you want me to tell you what
I should do myself if I were at once erring and repentant as you are? Shall I tell you to what I should
cling, to what sentiment, to what hope?"

"Tell me!"

"Listen: I should spend the rest of my life in
reparation for my fault by conduct totally the re-
verse of that which had rendered me so blameworthy
and so wretched. I should shut myself up in my
duty as in a cloister, win the love and blessing of
him whom I had had the misery of outraging in a
moment of aberration, endure every privation to
please him, exist only for him, consecrate and devote
myself to him utterly—do for him what a nun does
for God himself! And then, believe me, a day
would come when I should feel almost consoled and
forgiven!"

Her eyes glistened; she embraced me. "I believe you will save me," she said. "Yes, that seems
possible to me. Only, I cannot think any more;
my poor head is no longer capable of it. Then you
truly believe that I may see him again?"

"Without any doubt. You can, and you
ought."

She looked at me with the air of a frightened child, adding, "And embrace him?"

I bowed assent.

"I must leave for Paris to-morrow morning, then," she rejoined, "for he arrives at four o'clock."

"Yes, you must, dearest. It is all-important that you should be there at the moment of his return. I will take you to the station myself for the nine-o'clock train."

It was arranged thus: We were to invent a dispatch from M. d'Éblis to explain this unceremonious departure to Mme. de Louvercy. I insisted on conducting Cécile to her room; I helped her undress, and did not leave her till I saw her in bed. Worn out by such sustained excitement, she seemed to me calm and almost ready to go to sleep. I embraced her a last time, and went myself to seek some moments' repose, which I did not find.

Next day, a little before seven o'clock—it was hardly daylight—I rose and proceeded to Cécile's apartment. I knocked at the door of her room; there was no response. I entered. Two candles were flickering on the mantel. I went up to the bed; it was empty. Greatly astonished, I cast a rapid

glance around me. All her toilet of the evening
before, her dress, her fur cloak, her hat, were scattered about on the furniture where they had been
laid. In a corner of the room, her traveling-trunk
was open and the trays in disorder. I had noticed
the preceding evening, not without some surprise, a
light ball toilet, a dress of mauve silk, and Cécile
had told me that Julie, her maid, had stupidly put
it into the trunk by mistake. This dress was no
longer there. I felt a sort of vague terror, a semi-
stupor. I was about to ring, to call, when my eye
was caught by a letter placed conspicuously on the
chimney-piece, between the two lighted candles. I
seized it; it was addressed to me, and I recognized
Cécile's handwriting. I opened it, and this is what
I read:

"My well-beloved Charlotte, I can never see him
again. In spite of my sin, I am still too honest a
woman for that. I am going to die, my poor dearie.
Forgive me the trouble I cause you. I believe God,
in spite of everything, will receive me kindly, for
he sees what I suffer. I love life, oh! so much;
but there is no way, you see!

9

"I thought it all over yesterday evening coming from the station to the château. All along the road, looking at that deep snow covering all the country, I kept saying to myself that I would like to lie down in it and sleep forever. This is the death I have chosen. I have read somewhere that one does not suffer much; that when the first shock is over one sleeps gently. I hope that it will be thus with me.

"You know where you will find me, dearest. Do you remember my saying to you one day that I should like to be buried there? I do not believe that would be possible; but I want at least to die there. It was there that he told me he loved me—that he asked me if I would be his wife. Alas! yes; I was very glad to be, for I loved him so well, and I was so proud of his love—the love I have not known how to preserve and protect!

"Tell him everything. I desire it—I entreat you to. Tell him of my sin—my dishonor; but tell him also of my repentance, will you not?

"You are the one he ought to have loved; he ought to have chosen you; I always thought so. You, only, were worthy of him. I wish he may open his eyes at last; it is my last wish. You are both of you free—and, then, if you owe your happiness to me, you will have more pity—you will both more readily forgive your poor little dead

" Cécile."

This letter has very often been wet with my tears, but it was not then. I was wild. I had no longer thought, nor voice, nor tears. All at once, the idea that every moment lost would be irreparable roused me from my stupor. I ran to my room; I called one of my servants, Jean, my husband's old soldier, who had remained in my service, and who possessed my fullest confidence. I told him briefly that I had something to do in the park, and that I wanted him to accompany me. He was evidently struck with the change in my voice and the agitation of my features; but he asked no questions. I got myself ready; he was ready himself in a moment, and we went out of the château by the stable-door, so as to attract no attention.

I was forced to confide to this man all that I could tell him of the frightful truth. I began to give him on the way the explanation I had hastily

prepared. Mme. d'Éblis, I told him, had retired
the night before with a high fever, arising from the
fatigue of her journey through the snow; in her
wandering she had spoken to me of strange things,
as if in her sleep: that her head was on fire, that
she wanted to go out—to go into the park, to sleep
in the snow. Unhappily I had attached no importance to these feverish words, especially as I saw her
sink into a sound sleep; but this morning, when I
went to see how she was, I did not find her in her
room. I made sure that she was not in the château;
still other indications made me fear that her fever
had increased during the night, and that in a fit of
delirium she had attempted to carry out her sinister
dreams. We should go first to look for her footsteps in the retired part of the park which they
call the Hermitage. I supposed that in her wan-
derings she must have gone this way in spite of
herself, as this Hermitage had always been her
favorite walking-place. Finally, I had warned no
one but him, because I wished to spare Mme. de
Louvercy my fears so long as a ray of hope was
left me.

Jean had had at the first word an idea which did

not occur to me : he retraced his footsteps quickly
as far as the lodge, and sent the porter after the family physician. Then we resumed our march, which
the depth of the snow rendered very difficult, and
to me snail-like. Several roads which intersect in
the park lead from the château to the Hermitage.
We took the shortest. The surface of the snow
was uniform and undisturbed. A little hope ani-
mated my heart. But, at the turning of this first
avenue, Jean, who was in advance, stopped suddenly and uttered an exclamation. I ran up, and, with
inexpressible anguish, saw the repeated imprints of
two little feet, of two narrow and dainty boots,
which alone marred the uniformity of the white
plain. We looked at each other sadly. "Hurry,"
I said, in a low voice, and we hastened our march
still more. For a long time, alas! we followed
these footsteps amid the startling stillness of the
woods, under the gray, gloomy, and lowering sky of
that mournful winter morning. They led us almost
to the gateway of the park, then they turned abruptly and lost themselves in the path which runs through
the underbrush and comes out within a few steps of
the Hermitage.

" Madame is right," said Jean to me, in a whisper; " she is there." He saw that I stopped and was about to swoon; he begged me to lean on his arm. But that was impossible, the path being too narrow for us both. I passed by him and stepped forward. Yes, she was really there!

I have before described in these pages what this Hermitage glade was—its singular and poetic solitude, its groups of aged trees thinly scattered about, its little circular fountain, its air of a profound retreat; she was there. Issuing from the path, my first look fell on her. Still she could scarcely be seen. She was wrapped in her ghastly dress and her laces, her head raised a little against one of the tall beech-trees which shade the fountain. A little fresh snow had fallen in the night, and covered her like a kind of gauze. I remember also that from time to time light flakes fell from the branches above her head, and lit softly upon her.

I fell forward. " Cécile! Cécile!" I knelt down, took her in my arms, clasped her hand, colder than the snow itself. Nothing! Her heart beat no longer. The poor face was bluish. She was dead!

Ah! poor, dear child! It was then that I found my tears!

And yet I could not believe it; in spite of the sad affirmation of my companion, I still hoped. I remembered that there were some charcoal-burners' sheds at a little distance on the skirts of the woods and the park. I told Jean to try and carry her there; we could warm her—bring her back to life. The noble fellow, who was weeping like a child himself, raised her rigid form in his arms, and we directed our steps, I following him, toward these huts! What a march! What a scene! This desolate landscape!—this lovely dead girl, in festival attire! She had put it on, I have always thought, from a feeling of strange coquetry, to let her death harmonize with her life, and also, doubtless, that our last image of her should remain more touching, more gracious, and worthier of pity.

While the people of the huts pressed around her with me, I asked Jean to run to the château and bring the doctor, who must have arrived by that time. But why should I dwell on these sorrowful details? The doctor came only to confirm the terrible truth. Two hours later they bore her to the château. I repeated to my mother-in-law the explanation I had given to Jean, avoiding all idea of suicide: Cécile had had a fit of fever and delirium; she had gone out in her frenzy in the middle of the night; the cold had seized on her and killed her. The feverish state in which she had evidently been on the evening before lent a convincing appearance of truth to this explanation.

At noon a dispatch was sent to M. d'Éblis, to summon him in all haste; they said that his wife was very ill. He arrived in the evening. Mme. de Louvercy and I received him, and as soon as he saw us he understood that it was all over. He desired to be left alone with the poor body, and we heard him sobbing long and bitterly.

The next day but one Cécile was laid to rest forever in the little churchyard of Louvercy, next that very grave in which she was one day buried so full of life.

.   .   .   .

M. d'Éblis remained with us the rest of the week. We saw very little of him. He kept himself shut up in his room most of the time, or took long, solitary walks in the park. He was deeply absorbed, gloomy, and silent. He asked me no questions. He appeared to accept without hesitation, without a shadow of incredulity, the story I had invented to explain his wife's death, and which I had elaborated for him with such details as were fittest to make it appear plausible to him.

A month later, a few days after I had gone back to Paris, toward the middle of January, he came to see me for the first time after my return. After a few words of indifferent and embarrassed conversation, he got up, came toward me, and, touching my hand with his finger, said to me, " Tell me, madame, why did she kill herself?"

This shot took me completely by surprise, and I could not avoid confusion in my response :

" What!—but Cécile did not kill herself!"

" You are concealing it from me," he said, " you hid it from every one; but I am sure that she killed herself!"

" You are better informed than I, then," I said, " and that is impossible; I was there, and you were not."

" Pardon me," replied he; " but I know that all the details which you gave me concerning the cir-

202 THE DIARY OF A WOMAN.

cumstances which preceded this misfortune are imaginary. Thus, you strangely exaggerated the feverish state in which you left Cécile the night before.
Julie, her maid, entered the room once after you
had gone out, and found her sad and preoccupied,
but very calm. Hearing a noise, she went in a second time, a little after midnight. Cécile was up
and had put on her wrapper; she told this girl that
she was well, but that, being unable to sleep, she
was going to write to kill time till she grew drowsy;
she seemed to have been weeping, she was very
pale, but thoroughly mistress of her mind, her will,
and her language—no appearance of that delirium
which, according to you, drove her to an act of madness. You have deceived me, clearly. Oh! you
have excellent · reasons for it, I am sure; but she
killed herself. Why? Can you tell me?"

" Once more," replied I, with as much firmness
as I could muster, " I know nothing of this."

" So, you will not—you cannot tell me the reason
of her suicide?"

" If she committed suicide, I know not the
cause."

" You are unused to lying, poor woman. Very

well, pardon me. I do not wish to press you further. Besides, I know enough of it myself. She
killed herself the night before my return—before
seeing me again—so as not to see me again. If it
was thus, she did well."

How can I tell what was passing in my mind,
my heart, my conscience, during this terrible questioning? I had never had a thought of abusing
Cécile's last, feverish words by betraying the secret
of her sin ; but, since her husband had divined this
secret in spite of me, in spite of my sincerest efforts
to keep it from him, what ought I to do? I absolutely could not bring myself to betray and dishonor
her who had confided in me. I said to myself, too,
that I ought, by every means in my power, to spare
M. d'Éblis the bitterness, the degradation, the acute
sense of one of those outrages which to the honor
of a man are insupportable. I preferred to tear his
heart with a wholesome wound rather than humiliate
him, to add to its grief, perhaps, but at least to give
it no shame. More than all, if I let him believe in
Cécile's sin, he could not fail to make an active
search for her accomplice, to discover him, to engage him in a mortal quarrel—

"Well, monsieur," I said, resolutely, "do you really wish to know it? Yes, she killed herself. Why? I think I do in truth know, and you shall know also."

I opened my little boudoir writing-table and took out the letter which Cécile had sent me from Paris, after our short-lived quarrel, and a very few days before the fatal event. In this letter—which I have transcribed entire several pages back—she endeavored, it will be remembered, to excuse her remissness by that of her husband; she complained in the strongest terms of not being loved by him. With great apparent sincerity—which was, however, only apparent, as she soon after confessed to me—she told me she was very unhappy, tired of life and of being neglected, and ended with this cruelly equivocal phrase: "There are moments when my heart fails me, when my head is utterly lost, when I feel that I am ready for something desperate, some final and irreparable madness!"

I held out the letter to M. d'Éblis; he looked at the date, then read it, and, while he did so, his countenance writhed so that I almost repented what I had done. When he came to the end, his arms fell at his sides, and, raising his deeply troubled and hollow eyes toward me, he murmured, " My God, is this possible ! "

I dried my wet cheeks without replying.

He read that unhappy letter over again. Anxious that no doubt should recur to his mind, I riveted his conviction by telling him that Cécile had spent the evening preceding the catastrophe reiterating to me that she was at the end of her resources ; that she had fled from Paris the eve of his return, because she could not endure the thought of recommencing life with him under the burden of his alienation and aversion.   I added that I had exhausted every argument and endearment to calm her desperation, and that I had trusted in my success too lightly, since the misfortune had happened, after all.

" Then," cried he, in a choked voice, "it is I who have killed her ! "   He fell into a chair and remained for a long time with his face hidden in his hands, his tears trickling through his fingers.

I suffered horribly in witnessing this ; but, having only a choice between two evils, I felt convinced that I had spared him the bitterer one.

It was evening, and late. M. d'Éblis recovered a little from his first emotion, got up, thanked me in a gentle and affectionate tone for telling him the truth, however overwhelming it was to him, and left me.

It was two months ago to-day that this passed between us. The night that followed—every day and every night since—I asked myself if its consequences would not be what I had in no wise foreseen and, I confess, still less desired. I am going to explain myself here with utter sincerity. The first impression that Cécile's death made upon me was free from all personal after-thought; it was a blow which prostrated me and plunged me into a kind of dull despair. But I should not be believed if I dared to say that, when time had begun to exert its softening influence upon me, the thought that my union with M. d'Éblis had become possible never occurred to me. Cécile's last letter, her final adieu, were sufficient to recall it to me. We were both free, both entirely innocent of the sorrowful causes of our freedom. I did not feel in my own conscience, I could not imagine in his, any obstacle which could henceforth arise between us and separate two hearts which had been so long bound together by deep and mutual affection.

And still, since the day when I showed Cécile's letter to M. d'Éblis, to remove his suspicions, and when he came to believe himself the guilty cause of her suicide, I have been asking myself if I have not myself awakened in the conscience of this honorable man scruples of which I may become the victim. Has not his generous and sensitive soul, through my pious falsehood, felt the duty of expiation and, in some sort, of reparation toward her who is no more?

Surely I cannot desire that! But, unhappily, many indications lead me to believe it—the extreme reserve of M. d'Éblis toward me, his rare visits, his enduring and even increasing anguish.

This, then, is the truly solemn, truly heavy trial which I am undergoing, or which menaces me. And in this momentous time it is that the thought has occurred to me, that I have felt the need of recalling to myself without dissimulation or reticence all the events of my life since the very day of my marriage. I have taken up this journal again, told it everything, confided all to it, hoping to find therein inspiration for the course I must pursue. Alas! in veriest truth I find nothing—not an act, not a sentiment, not a thought, which should fetter the freedom God has given back to me, nothing which should prevent me from accepting the happiness I dreamed of long ago, which has so long been refused me, and which finally seems vouchsafed me.

But he? Ah, I still hope that his attitude, his silence, are accounted for by the increased suffering I believed it my duty to inflict upon him, by his bereavement, which is still so fresh; by the sense of propriety which actuates him. Yes, I hope this; but what if at last I should be mistaken? If the falsehood that I have risked to save Cécile's honor and spare his should rise up between us—and that alone separate us? What should I do then? I dare not think.

Eight hours later, March 20, 1878.

Nothing more is lacking to my burden. It is complete, it is pitiless.

M. d'Éblis came this evening just as I had put my daughter to bed. He asked to see me alone. I received him in my boudoir. As he seated himself before me he said, "Madame, I am going to leave you, I am going away."

"Away!" I cried.

"Yes. I have obtained the position of second military *attaché* in Russia. I leave to-morrow evening. I shall ask your permission to return to-morrow morning to bid good-by to my little pupil, whom I do not wish to awaken to-night."

I was overwhelmed. For several minutes I could not articulate an intelligible word.

Presently he resumed, in a very low voice: "We have always understood each other so well, we two, that I am sure we shall still understand each other now. When you revealed to me the true cause of Cécile's suicide, I understood at once, knowing you so well, the duty you imposed on me. I understood that you bade me love and respect in death her whom I misconceived in life. That is, indeed, what you wish, is it not? I obey you; but, to have strength to do so, I must go away, I must leave you."

I did not reply. He rose. "Good-by, then; I have loved you well. I can say that I have loved you more than my honor even; for—you will be-

lieve me vile—when I thought I had discovered Cécile's infidelity, and that, to kill her remorse, she
had killed herself, dreadful as the thought was, my
wretched heart nevertheless welcomed it with secret
joy, for it released me from her, it returned me to
you!"

As he was uttering these words, the unhappy
man still interrogated me with a look of doubt and
anguish.

I slew myself.

He grasped my hand and went out.

But yet—let me reflect—can I let him go? Is
it possible? Ought I? Can I? Oh, my God, tell
me! I have loved him so much. O God! I do
love him so much! And to let him go into exile—
perhaps to death—when by a single word I can keep
him forever at my side! He will believe me if I
tell him the truth; besides, I have that last note of
Cécile's; the confession of her fault written by her
own hand. She herself gave me permission, even
commanded me to deliver it to her husband. Oh,
it is unjust, after all; and we two have sacrificed
ourselves long enough! Happiness is there, and
nothing separates us from it any longer but an exag-

gerated, sickly, even mad scruple! No, I *will not* let him go; I have decided.

. . . .

All night long I sat up, pondering it all. All night long I saw the dear little friend of my childhood in her bed of snow, and I swore to do for her what I would have had her do for me: to protect her memory even to the end, even at the expense of my happiness, even at the cost of my life, to defend her honor at any price—to leave her, my poor little dead girl, pure and white in the memory of all! Sleep in peace, darling. Only God and myself shall know your fault!

I have just burned her funereal letter—the sole proof.

I have written to M. d'Éblis, praying him to spare me his last adieu. I shall see him no more. I am alone, alone forever!

But you are left to me, my daughter. I write these last lines at the side of your cradle. I hope some day to put these pages in your bridal trousseau, my child; perhaps they will lead you to love your poor, romantic mother; you will learn of her, perhaps, that passion and romance are good sometimes, with God's assistance; that they elevate the heart; that they teach it higher duties, great sacrifices, the noblest joys of life. My tears fall as I tell it you, it is true; but, believe me, there are tears which the angels envy.

THE END.

APPLETONS'

NEW HANDY-VOLUME SERIES.

Brilliant Novelettes; Romance, Adventure, Travel, Humor;

Historic, Literary, and Society Monographs.

I.

JET: Her Face or her Fortune? By Mrs. ANNIE EDWARDES, author of "Archie Lovell," "Ought we to visit Her?" etc. 30 cents.

"'Jet' is a thoroughly good book. It is pure in purpose, fresh and attractive in style, and fully justifies all the 'great expectations' based upon the reputation Mrs. Edwardes has gained for herself."—*Boston Post.*

II.

A STRUGGLE. By BARNET PHILLIPS. 25 cents.

"A charming novelette of the Franco-German War, told in a pleasant and interesting manner that absorbs the mind until the story is finished."—*Philadelphia Times.*

III.

MISERICORDIA. By ETHEL LYNN LINTON. 20 cents.

"We are not sure that we like anything by Mrs. Linton better than this."—*New York Evening Post.*

IV.

GORDON BALDWIN, and THE PHILOSOPHER'S PENDULUM. By RUDOLPH LINDAU. 25 cents.

"Both tales are full of dramatic interest, and both are told with admirable skill."—*New York Evening Post.*

"We recommend to readers of fiction these two remarkable stories."—*New York Times.*

V.

THE FISHERMAN OF AUGE. By KATHARINE S. MACQUOID. 20 cents.

"A particularly good bit of work by Katharine S. Macquoid. The story has a strong plot, and some of its scenes are fine bits of dramatic writing."—*New York Evening Post.*

VI.

ESSAYS OF ELIA. First Series. By CHARLES LAMB. 30 cents.

"The quaintness of thought and expression, the originality and humor and exquisite elaboration of the papers, have made them as much a standard as any of the writings of Addison and Steele, and far more agreeable."—*Philadelphia North American.*

VII.

THE BIRD OF PASSAGE. By J. SHERIDAN LE FANU, author of "Uncle Silas," etc. 25 cents.

"The heroine is a pleasant relief from the crowd of conventional beauties that one knows by heart. The scenes of the book are as odd as the characters."—*Boston Courier.*

VIII.

THE HOUSE OF THE TWO BARBELS. By ANDRÉ THEURIET, author of "Gérard's Marriage," "The Godson of a Marquis," etc. 20 cents.

"The tale is pretty, and so naïvely and charmingly told, with such delicate yet artistic characterization, that it leaves a most delightful impression on the reader's mind."—*New York Express.*

"A delightful little romance, exquisite in its conception and perfect in its style."—*Philadelphia Record.*

"The character of Germain Lafrogne is one of the best in modern fiction."—*Baltimore Sun.*

IX.

LIGHTS OF THE OLD ENGLISH STAGE. Biographical and Anecdotical Sketches of Famous Actors of the Old English Stage. Reprinted from *Temple Bar.* 30 cents.

"The book treats of Richard Burbage and other 'originals' of Shakespeare's characters, the Cibbers, Garrick, Charles Macklin, 'Peg' Woffington and George Anne Bellamy, John Kemble and Mrs. Siddons, Cooke, Edmund Kean, Charles Young, Dora Jordan, and Mrs. Robinson. A more interesting group of persons it would be hard to find."—*New York World.*

X.

IMPRESSIONS OF AMERICA. From the *Nineteenth Century*. By R. W. DALE. I. Society. II. Politics. III. and IV. Popular Education. 30 cents.

"Mr. Dale's chapter upon American politics shows a greater degree of fairness and a better understanding of the spirit of our institutions than are exhibited by most English writers. In speaking of our social characteristics, he says that during the whole of his stay, and in all parts of the country, East and West, he was struck 'with the extreme gentleness of American manners,' and gives several instances which came under his observation."—*Boston Evening Transcript.*

"The book shows how our society, politics, and systems of popular education, strike an intelligent, observing, fair-minded foreigner. The style of the book is pleasant, and the writer notices our republican ways with a mingling of surprise, admiration, and amusement, that is refreshing to read about."—*Louisville Courier-Journal.*

XI.

THE GOLDSMITH'S WIFE. By Madame CHARLES REYBAUD. 25 cents.

"No one but a woman could have sounded the depths of the nature of this goldsmith's wife, and portrayed so clearly her exquisite purity and the hard struggles she underwent."—*New York Mail.*

"The simplicity and delicacy of this little story render it as unique as it is exquisite."—*Albany Argus.*

XII.

A SUMMER IDYL. By CHRISTIAN REID, author of "Bonny Kate," "Valerie Aylmer," etc. 30 cents.

"A Summer Idyl" is a charming summer sketch, the scene of which is on the French Broad, in North Carolina. It is eminently entertaining as a story, as well as a delightful idyllic rural picture.

"We consider it one of Christian Reid's best efforts. It is full of spirit and adventure, relieved by an exquisite love-episode."—*Philadelphia Item.*

XIII.

THE ARAB WIFE. A Romance of the Polynesian Seas. 25 cents.

"The Arab Wife" is a picturesque and romantic story, of a kind to recall to many readers those brilliant books of thirty years ago—Melville's "Typee" and "Omoo."

XIV.

MRS. GAINSBOROUGH'S DIAMONDS. By JULIAN HAWTHORNE, author of "Bressant," "Garth," etc. 20 cents.

"This interesting little story fully sustains the reputation of Julian Hawthorne. In him, at least, we have one more proof of the 'heredity of genius.'"

XV.

LIQUIDATED, and THE SEER. By RUDOLPH LINDAU, author of "Gordon Baldwin" and "The Philosopher's Pendulum." 25 cents.

"Rudolph Lindau is a young German author, rising rapidly to fame, whose stories have principally Americans and Englishmen for their *dramatis personæ*, and are remarkable for dramatic directness and force, insight into character, and freshness of motive and incident."

XVI.

THE GREAT GERMAN COMPOSERS. Comprising Biographical and Anecdotical Sketches of Bach, Handel, Gluck, Haydn, Mozart, Beethoven, Schubert, Schumann, Franz, Chopin, Weber, Mendelssohn, and Wagner. 30 cents.

XVII.

ANTOINETTE. A Story. By ANDRÉ THEURIET. 20 cents.

"Theuriet is the envied author of several graceful novelettes, artistic and charming, of which 'Antoinette' is not the least delightful."—*Boston Post.*

XVIII.

JOHN–A–DREAMS. A Tale. 30 cents.

"A capital little story; spirited in the telling, bright in style, and clever in construction."—*Boston Gazette.*

XIX.

MRS. JACK. A Story. By FRANCES ELEANOR TROLLOPE. 20 cents.

"It is a well-written story, and will generally be voted too short. The characters are vividly imagined and clearly realized, while the author has a sense of humor which lightens the work."—*Philadelphia Inquirer.*

XX.

ENGLISH LITERATURE, from 596 to 1832. By T. ARNOLD. Reprinted from the "Encyclopædia Britannica." 25 cents.

"Emphatically a history of intellectual ideas rather than a tedious catalogue of books and authors. Scarcely any notable book or author is omitted."—*N. Y. Even'g Express.*

XXI.

RAYMONDE. A Tale. By ANDRÉ THEURIET, author of "Gérard's Marriage," etc. 30 cents.

"A story well planned, well written, and not long. It is bright, readable, and unexceptionable in its tone and inculcations."—*Worcester Spy.*

XXII.

BEACONSFIELD. A Sketch of the Literary and Political Career of Benjamin Disraeli, now Earl of Beaconsfield. With Two Portraits. By GEORGE M. TOWLE. 25 cents.

*** Any volume mailed, post-paid, to any address within the United States, on receipt of the price.

D. APPLETON & CO., PUBLISHERS, 549 & 551 BROADWAY, NEW YORK.

www.ingramcontent.com/pod-product-compliance
Lightning Source LLC
Chambersburg PA
CBHW020610030726
47497CB00007B/2169